The Center of Change

Tara Howard

Chapter 1

Jessica

"But Mom," I yelled from my small bedroom, my voice echoing off the pastel walls adorned with posters of cheerful landscapes and whimsical quotes, "it's not fair! Jenna didn't have to participate in the center competitions."

Yet, deep down, I understood the harsh reality of our situation all too well. Our nation had enacted a law long ago, a cruel measure designed to regulate the population and safeguard the interests of the wealthy elite. Families from lower socioeconomic backgrounds, if they dared to have more than one child of the same gender, faced a heart-wrenching choice: terminate the pregnancy or send the second child to the centers upon turning 18. My sister

Jenna, fortunate enough to be the eldest, would be married off to another family of low status—a fate that felt almost like a reprieve in comparison to what awaited me. Meanwhile, my younger brother Joshua was set to inherit our father's furniture-making business, a stable future that seemed so tantalizingly distant for me. As for me, I was bound for the centers, the ominous specter looming over my future. The best I could hope for was to catch a final glimpse of my parents if I managed to triumph in the center assigned to me and somehow marry into status.

Otherwise, the center-hunters had two grim alternatives awaiting me. The first option was a dreaded re-entry into a new center to compete again—an exceedingly rare scenario usually reserved for top competitors or those claimed as spouses by the elite. The second option was even worse: I could end up as a servant or laborer for either the affluent or the government, a life of servitude that loomed ominously in my mind like an inescapable shadow. I had been raised to brace for the psychological battles of the centers, but I had never truly decided which path I desired the most, caught between fear and hope.

"Jessica," my mother's voice was tender and soothing, cutting through the turmoil in my heart like a warm blanket on a cold night. "I am so sorry this is happening. I genuinely believed these laws would have changed before you turned 18." She gently ran her fingers through my hair, the familiar touch comforting me as she pulled me into a warm embrace, an anchor amidst the chaotic storm of my emotions.

I was born just a year before my aunt had triumphed in a center, marrying a man far from here, a life that felt like a fairy tale. Her final words to my mother on her wedding day had been, "I promise I will change this, for Jess."

Tragically, she passed away in a car accident a year later, never realizing that dream, leaving a gaping hole in our family that still ached, a reminder of what could have been.

I leaned against the cool wall of my bedroom, memories of Aunt Clara flooding my mind like a river bursting its banks. My mother's younger voice still echoed in the corners of my thoughts, her stories weaving a tapestry of what life could have been— what it should have been.

"Clara was so brave," Mom said, her eyes shimmering with unshed tears. "She never backed down from a challenge. Even when they were sending her to the center." She explained her so in depth that I could picture Clara standing tall, head held high, the sun catching her golden hair like a halo. She fought fiercely for what she believed in, determined to carve out a better future not just for herself but for those she loved.

Mom told me about Clara's life as a child, how she outshone everyone else with her intelligence and tenacity. The way she navigated the cutthroat second- born childhood was nothing short of legendary among our family. She had plans to change things— real change that could've altered our lives forever.

"Your aunt always believed in second chances," Mom had said, wiping away a tear that betrayed her stoic demeanor. "She wanted to create a world where families didn't have to lose their children."

A knot twisted in my stomach as I recalled those stories—the hope and light they carried mixed with an unbearable sadness. Clara's dreams vanished like smoke after her tragic death, leaving behind whispers of what might have been.

The more I thought about it, the more anger bubbled up inside me. Why did Clara fight so hard only to have it all snatched away? And here I was, about to face the same fate she had bravely battled against. Did her courage mean anything if I couldn't live up to it?

In moments like these, I felt the weight of expectations pressing down on me—a burden heavier than any backpack full of schoolbooks. Jenna lived in this bubble of perfection, shielded from everything while I prepared myself for something dark and uncharted. I craved adventure and love yet found myself trapped by rules that bound my heart and soul.

"Jess?" Mom's voice broke through my reverie. Her worried gaze searched mine as if trying to read the pages of my heart's unwritten story.

I sank deeper into my mom's embrace, tears streaming down my cheeks as I wept through my words, "It's okay, momma. I love you, just make sure everyone here is alright without me." With those words, we both wept into each other, our shared grief mingling in the air like a tangible entity, heavy with unspoken fears and regrets.

We held each other tightly for at least ten minutes before my mom pulled away, resolute, to continue packing my belongings, her movements steady but tinged with sadness.

I flopped onto my bed, the soft comforter a stark contrast to the turmoil inside me, and grabbed my phone, desperate for a distraction. Scrolling through pictures of myself with my best friends, Mia and Grace, I felt a pang of nostalgia stab at my heart. Both Mia and Grace were set to enter centers within the next month, and the thought sent shivers down my spine, leaving an icy knot in my stomach. When we were younger, the three of us would dream about losing together and being assigned to serve the same family, imagining a bond that would somehow shield us from the harsh realities ahead. Back then, it didn't seem so terrible; we were blissfully unaware of the stark realities of the rich or that they never truly had a day off. But after hitting puberty, it became painfully evident that Mia was too attractive for her own good. If she didn't win, she would likely become a professional surrogate, producing heirs for the wealthy who couldn't, or worse, a sex slave for government officials or a wealthy man who ended up with a winner he didn't want. Grace and I worried about the opposite.

Neither of us considered ourselves particularly appealing, and we feared becoming the wives of men who despised our presence, a fate that felt like a prison, a gilded cage with no escape.

My greatest fear, however, was losing the ability to think for myself, to be silenced by the oppressive weight of expectation that loomed over me like a dark cloud. My teachers had always lamented that it was unfortunate I was born second, a sentiment that felt like both a curse and a compliment. They recognized my intelligence, noting that I was smarter than average, and yet that very trait often led me to question adults when they were wrong. It was a double-edged sword; they seemed to both admire my curiosity and fear the consequences it might invoke. After a humiliating public reprimand by an enforcer, who made an example of me when I dared to point out a flaw in a news brief, I quickly realized that my intellect was my biggest adversary in the world I was destined to enter. It was a world that punished those who dared to challenge authority, where questioning was seen not as an opportunity for growth but as an act of defiance. I felt the sting of shame wash over me in that moment, a reminder that in standing up for what I believed to be right, I had only succeeded in drawing the ire of those who held power. It was a bitter lesson, one that left me grappling with the knowledge that the very thing that made me unique could also be the source of my undoing.

As I was growing up, I often felt like a mere shadow, hidden behind the dazzling glow of my sister's fortune. Jenna didn't intend to eclipse me; she was just the perfect daughter, a title bestowed upon her like a crown, effortlessly. I can still recall the way her teachers extolled her virtues, showering her with accolades that fell down like confetti. However, as the second born, I soon understood that my presence was accompanied by constraints—like a frustrating case of being the second violin in an orchestra where everyone else played their instruments worse than I did.

When it came time for secondary school, I was forced to attend a special school for second- borns. "For your own good," they said, but deep down, I sensed the truth—the world wanted to keep us down. I needed to learn how to navigate a world designed for those who mattered. While Jenna joined clubs and made friends effortlessly, I shuffled into classrooms filled with other kids deemed unworthy of attention. We hung out together in our free time, exchanging whispered dreams about escaping our fates while stealing glances at those who roamed freely outside our little bubble.

Every trip around town felt like a reminder of my place in society. At businesses, I entered through the side doors—the "service entrance"—while the rest of my family glided through the main entrance without a second thought. Those moments cut deep, feeling the judgmental eyes on me as I slipped away from everyone else. Sometimes I'd watch people walk past the main doors, laughter spilling out like sunshine, and wonder what it felt like to belong there.

"Hey Jess," Grace would say with an edge of defiance in her voice during one of those long walks home after school. "We are not just some nobody." She had this way of making me believe for a split second that maybe we weren't just destined for second-class status.

But those moments never lasted long. Reality hit hard when we learned that society treated children based on perceived value—a cruel metric where being born first of the gender equated to importance and privilege. It was more than just societal norms; it was a cold truth woven into every interaction and choice made around us.

Even as we sat in our small town diner—the only place willing to serve all—waitresses treated us differently. They barely masked their disdain when they served me compared to how warmly they greeted Jenna and Joshua.

Each interaction left its mark, reminding me that no matter how smart or talented I might be, I would always be seen as less than enough—a flicker of light drowned out by someone else's glow.

Mom finished packing my fourteen perfectly coordinated outfits—each one a carefully chosen reflection of my personality—and zipped my duffel bag before enveloping me in another heartfelt embrace. "I truly am sorry, baby girl. I hope you understand how much this is breaking my heart," she murmured, her voice thick with emotion, trembling slightly as she spoke. I could see the pain etched on her face, the way her eyes glistened with unshed tears, and it made my chest tighten. It was as if every word she uttered carried the weight of a thousand unspoken fears, and I couldn't help but feel the ache of her sorrow intertwining with my own.

I returned her hug, holding on tightly as if I could absorb her strength before reluctantly opening the door to let her out. "I know, mom. It's not your fault our world is completely messed up," I replied, my voice a mixture of sadness and resilience, trying to reassure both her and myself in the face of our uncertain future.

∞∞∞∞

The following morning, I quietly slipped out of the house before anyone had a chance to stir, careful to leave behind a note that would prevent my parents from worrying about my sudden absence.

At the bus stop, I spotted Mia and Grace waiting for me, their expressions a mix of concern and camaraderie. I must have looked a bit rough around the edges, because Mia's first remark was, "Shit... not looking forward to this, are you?"

I chuckled softly, wrapping my arms around her in a warm embrace. "Losing my life as I know it? Ummm, not exactly my top pick for tomorrow."

"Maybe there will be a charming guy. Your knight in shining armor?" Grace teased lightly as the bus rolled in, its engine humming steadily in the morning air.

We began to talk animatedly about what the center might be like, jumping from one topic to another— what competitions I was hoping to face and which ones I dreaded the most. Our training had been intense, years of preparation for a reality that loomed before us like a dark cloud. I felt a knot tighten in my stomach as I thought of the timed block game, where you had to stack blocks rapidly while trying to maintain your balance on a wobbly board. I found that game not just challenging, but awful and utterly pointless. Instead, I wished they had a memory game; I excelled at remembering things, especially short-term ones. Mia, on the other hand, was fond of the scavenger hunts, her eyes lighting up at the thought of searching for hidden treasures. Grace and I both agreed, however, that the endurance challenges, where you had to cling desperately to a dangling pole, were the most physically demanding and grueling of all.

But deeper than all that, I was mostly fearful of the emotional manipulation that awaited us. I knew all too well that people would deceive, cheat, and steal from each other in a desperate bid to get ahead. My heart raced at the thought; I had no clue who to trust aside from my own instincts. The rules were strict—I could only have two contacts in my phone while at the center, and my communications would be monitored closely. The facility itself was under constant surveillance by cameras, their unblinking lenses capturing every moment. There were insidious rumors that the affluent and influential kept a watchful eye on the proceedings, often selecting who would be given a chance to return when they failed or who would fill the roles at their centers.

"I've chosen you two as my outside contacts," I proclaimed excitedly over ice cream at our favorite spot, looking into their faces for reassurance and support. It was highly unusual to make such a choice; typically, family members—usually parents or siblings —were selected, sometimes a boyfriend or girlfriend. Occasionally, a wealthy or powerful friend would be chosen to facilitate their entry into the staff upon expulsion from the center.

"You can do that?" Mia exclaimed, her eyes wide with surprise and disbelief.

I nodded confidently. "There's nothing stating I can't. The only rule is that I cannot reach out to you AFTER I enter the center."

"But how can we assist you? We're heading to centers next, just like you," Grace interjected, her brow furrowing with concern.

I smiled at them, feeling a warmth spread through me. "You'll help keep me sane. And hopefully, I'll manage to attract some positive attention from the wealthy before you even arrive at the center."

With that, I sprang up from our booth, tossing away my trash with a newfound energy before leaving the shop. The two of them sat in stunned silence, absorbing the gravity of our situation as I stepped out into the world beyond.

∞∞∞∞

After a few lengthy embraces, I returned home to find my family gathered in the living room, where a tall, formal auburn-haired businesswoman stood poised and confident.

"Hello, Jessica," she welcomed me with an unexpected warmth that seemed at odds with her polished demeanor.

"I'm Camilla, the center hunter assigned to be your handler. I've truly enjoyed getting to know your family; they're quite charming."

I couldn't help but notice the telltale signs that Jenna had been crying—her red-rimmed eyes and the faint quiver of her lips. Protectively, I shot back, "Why do they have to be part of this?"

Camilla grinned, her expression playful. "Feisty little one, aren't you? This should be quite entertaining." She assessed me from head to toe like I was a mannequin in a department store, her gaze appraising every detail before pulling out a notebook. "About 5'3", long blonde hair, green eyes. What do you weigh, 140?"

I rolled my eyes in exasperation. "115 pounds, and I'm 5'4". Not that it matters," I replied, crossing my arms defensively.

Camilla shook her head, her gaze locking onto mine with an intensity that made me uncomfortable as she continued to write. "It seems they may have given me some potential this time, if you can learn a bit of decorum," she remarked, her tone almost challenging.

Before I could muster a retort, my mom stood up, her nervous energy palpable. "Camilla, would you like to see Jessica's room?" she asked, eager to change the subject.

The next two hours blurred together in a whirlwind of activity as I guided Camilla through my life. I opened my wardrobe for her inspection, displayed my collection of jewelry, detailed my hair routine, and finally posed for the "center hunters directory."

Camilla's inquiries were relentless; she wanted to know everything from my skills training to my sexual history. A hint of satisfaction crossed her face when she learned I was a virgin, as she claimed it would make me more appealing to male employers. Her delight only grew when I shared my impressive IQ test results. As we continued our conversation, she took copious notes while chattering about how female employers would likely view me with disdain. Camilla advised me to always wear makeup, never to flirt with any men, and emphasized that if I wanted even the slightest chance at success, I needed to appeal to the men who would be observing my every move.

Camilla plopped down on my bed, her sharp gaze sweeping over the posters of my favorite bands, a mix of disdain and amusement dancing across her features. "You can't keep this clutter," she declared, flicking her fingers dismissively toward a pile of clothes that had been hastily tossed aside. "We need to create an image that speaks sophistication and readiness for the center. People who find you interesting may come to see your family and learn more about you; this," she gestured broadly at my room, "will not get you much interest."

A frown creased my brow, reluctant to part with the pieces of my world that held so much meaning. "It's just me. I like music and art," I protested, my voice tinged with defiance.

"Music and art don't get you anywhere in this game," she snapped back, her pen tapping rhythmically against her notebook like a metronome counting down the seconds of my youthful rebellion. "We need to curate your life like a gallery. Every detail matters."

Without warning, she began tossing clothes onto the floor—my beloved band tee, a well-worn hoodie—like they were worthless scraps of paper. My heart raced, and I clenched my fists, fighting the urge to scream in frustration.

"Those are mine!" I blurted out, stepping forward as if to reclaim my belongings.

Camilla met my gaze coolly, her expression unyielding. "If you want them in your life, fine. But remember: what you wear sends a message." With that, she pulled out a sleek black dress from my closet, holding it up against me as if it were a prized trophy. "This is more like it."

"Do I really have to wear that?" My voice came out weaker than I intended, betraying my uncertainty.

"Absolutely," she replied with finality, a sense of authority emanating from her. She pushed me toward the bathroom with a firm hand on my back. "Get changed. We don't have all day."

I reluctantly slipped into the dress, the fabric clinging uncomfortably to my curves, making me acutely aware of every inch of my body. Staring at myself in the mirror, I hardly recognized the girl looking back— too polished, too grown-up. The reflection felt like a stranger, one I wasn't sure I wanted to become.

"Much better," Camilla said as she entered behind me, her eyes sparkling with satisfaction. She positioned herself like a director surveying her set, ready to mold my image to her vision. "Now let's fix that hair."

I watched as she gathered supplies from my vanity— a curling iron, brushes, and an array of hair products that looked more at home in a salon than my cozy bedroom. The scent of hairspray filled the air, a stark reminder of the transformation I was undergoing.

"Hold still." Her hands worked deftly as she curled sections of hair away from my face, the heat from the iron brushing against my neck, sending tingles down my spine.

"What's wrong with how I usually do it?" I asked, trying to hold onto a shred of my individuality.

She paused for a moment, shooting me an exasperated look over her shoulder, her patience wearing thin. "It's not about what you like anymore; it's about what they want." Her tone was matter-of- fact, devoid of the warmth I so desperately craved.

"What if they don't like me?" I asked, the vulnerability in my voice betraying my bravado.

She sighed dramatically but continued curling with practiced precision, her hands moving expertly through my hair. "That's not an option you can afford. You need to be likable; it's your ticket to the world you want."

The heat from the iron pressed against my neck as I stared at myself again, transforming slowly under Camilla's watchful eye, each curl and stroke reshaping not just my hair but my entire identity. When it was finally time for her to leave, her excitement was almost palpable. "You are just the diamond in the rough that we need," she declared, her eyes sparkling with enthusiasm. "Play your cards right, and you won't be condemned to a life of misery.

Chapter 2

Jessica

After some tearful farewells the following morning, a lengthy flight, and a two-hour drive, I found myself approaching the center. "It's Showtime!" Camilla yelled at me from the sidewalk, her voice cutting through the swirl of my nerves like a knife through butter, and for a moment, I felt a flicker of excitement amidst the anxiety.

My heart raced as I opened the door to the center. The sound of chatter on the other side was overwhelming, a cacophony of voices mingling together, making it painfully obvious that I was one of the last arrivals to this chaotic beginning. Taking a deep breath to steady my nerves, I rolled my suitcase in quietly, hoping desperately to slip in unnoticed and find my footing in this whirlwind of unfamiliarity.

I glanced toward the living room. An attractive blonde guy was chatting loudly with two girls around a table, their laughter punctuating the air in a way that made my stomach twist a little. They were hanging on his every word, leaning in close as if he were sharing the secrets of the universe. One of the girls, a blonde adorned with multiple piercings and at least one visible tattoo, reached out to grab his hand while emitting a clearly phony laugh that echoed in my ears, grating against my nerves.

Her companion, a brunette with perfectly straight hair and model-like features, exuded an air of confidence that made her the undeniable star of the duo. I rolled my eyes, mentally noting to steer clear of them; they looked like trouble wrapped in pretty packaging.

"Hey! Welcome to the shitshow!" a cheerful voice called from the kitchen, breaking my train of thought and drawing my attention away from the chaos in the living room. I spotted a girl with dirty blonde hair preparing something that smelled absolutely amazing, the aroma wafting through the air and making my stomach grumble in response, reminding me that I hadn't eaten since yesterday.

I strolled over and hopped onto a barstool, eager to engage with someone who seemed friendly amidst the sea of unfamiliar faces. "I'm Jessica. Nice to meet you," I said with a smile, hoping to make a good impression and perhaps find an ally in this new environment.

"I'm Carolynn." She extended a hand across the kitchen island, which I gladly shook, appreciating her warmth and the genuine kindness radiating from her. "The lovesick puppy is Allison, and that's her shadow, Paige. They came in together; I think they probably knew each other before arriving." She shared some details about the girls lounging on the couch, her tone dripping with a mix of amusement and exasperation that made me feel a little more at ease.

"And who are they swooning over?" I asked candidly, unable to resist the urge to dig deeper. If I wanted to last long here, I needed to know my competition, the players in this strange game.

Carolynn winked at me, a conspiratorial glint in her eyes that made me feel like I was sharing a secret. "That's Eric. He looks all muscle, but I don't know much about him yet." She returned to her cooking, her hands skillfully chopping vegetables with a precision that made me momentarily envious. "Do you like Mexican food?"

"Absolutely, margaritas included?" I laughed, feeling a spark of excitement as I jumped up from my stool, ready to dive into this new adventure. "I'm going to unpack, and I'll be back."

I wandered into the bedroom, the scent of fresh linens mingling with the air, offering a slight comfort amidst the chaos. It was a spacious room with twelve beds and twelve lockers, an odd mix of cozy and chaotic that made my heart race anew. I located the locker with my name on it and began to unpack, trying to settle in and calm my racing thoughts. While I was doing so, a sweet, bookish girl named Leslie approached to introduce herself. Apparently, her locker and bed were next to mine—a small comfort in this overwhelming place. She showed me to my bed before climbing into hers and curling up with a book, her sanctuary amid the noise. "I like to read; it calms my nerves," she smiled at me before turning to her reading, her quiet presence a welcome contrast to the bustling energy outside our room, grounding me just a little in this whirlwind of new experiences.

The twelve of us gathered around the dinner table, each of us nibbling on burritos and sipping margaritas, the atmosphere thick with an uncomfortable silence that felt endless. It was Carolynn who eventually shattered the stillness, her voice a gentle prompt. "Why don't we go around and introduce ourselves?" A wave of nods swept across the table, a collective decision to fill the quiet with conversation.

"My family are pig farmers," Carolynn started, her voice steady, though her eyes revealed the emotions swirling inside her. "I grew up on a farm with my older sister and twin brother. My sister is a teacher now." As she spoke, I noticed a hint of tears threatening to escape, and I felt a pang of compassion for her. It was evident that her past held significant meaning for her, even if the memories carried a touch of sorrow.

The circle continued, each person sharing fragments of their experiences. Eric, the muscular blonde who exuded confidence, proclaimed his passion for sports, which was no surprise to any of us. Allison, ever the instigator, managed to weave in about five sexual innuendos into her story, eliciting a few chuckles from the group. Then there was Leslie, whose parents owned the only bank in her town, her voice soft and literary as she recounted her tale.

When my turn arrived, a wave of anxiety washed over me. I wanted to come across as ordinary, to provide them nothing they could hold against me. I inhaled deeply and smiled politely. "Hey, I'm Jess. I'm nothing remarkable. I have an older sister, Jenna, and a younger brother, Joshua. My family are furniture makers, and I enjoy writing." My goal was to stay under the radar, and thankfully, it seemed successful; no one focused much on me as the stories continued.

The last to speak was a sweet girl named Dot, sitting beside Carolynn. She began sharing her story, explaining that her parents had enrolled her to become a nun, claiming that God had summoned her. It was a grim reality for many second children like us, the only alternative to the Centers. But as she spoke, she revealed that during the vetting process, it was discovered she had kissed a boy at the tender age of ten, and just like that, she was expelled from the program. We all leaned in, captivated by her narrative. The nunnery program was notorious for its harshness, with chilling tales of corporal punishment and even death for those who dared to defy the rules once they were deemed nuns.

"Shit," the exclamation slipped from my mouth before I could stop it, and suddenly, all eyes were on me. A moment of silence followed before the room erupted in laughter, the tension shattering like a fragile bubble.

Allison, ever sharp, took the chance. "So are you really called to God? Like, you don't want a real man ever between those legs?" Her teasing tone was playful yet pointed, and Dot's face flushed a deep shade of red as her eyes darted around, searching for a way out of the spotlight.

"Cut the crap," a young guy interjected, his voice slicing through the laughter. I hadn't caught his name, but his tone was serious. "We know the rules about lying in that program. No one needs to risk Dot's life. It's not like here where they welcome it if we deceive one another."

With that, the lighthearted banter faded away, and the group fell into an uneasy silence, clearing the dishes and tidying up the remnants of our meal. After the last plate was washed, I excused myself, fatigue pulling at my limbs. I had a competition to prepare for in the morning, and I needed to be at my best.

As I settled into bed, I quickly sent a text to Mia and Grace, my two closest friends who always seemed to know how to lift my spirits:

Jessica: "I'm here. No knights in shining armor to rescue me. It's okay."

Mia: "Screw the knights. You're brilliant."

Grace: "Wait... who is screwing the knights?"

I chuckled softly at their playful banter, warmth spreading through me as I sank into the comfort of my blankets, finally allowing the day to slip away.

Bright lights and a loudspeaker jolted me awake from the depths of my deep sleep, a sudden intrusion that felt almost shocking against the backdrop of my dreams.

"You have 30 minutes to find all the puzzle pieces. The winner stays another day; others may be booted," the robotic voice blared through the loudspeaker, echoing in my ears as it repeated the same urgent message. "You have 30 minutes to find all the puzzle pieces. The winner stays another day; others may be booted."

"Shit," I mumbled, the reality of the situation hitting me like a cold splash of water. I rolled out of bed, my heart racing as I quickly ran my fingers through my hair, trying to tame the wild strands that had tangled during the night, and I straightened my pajamas, which felt a bit rumpled from my restless sleep.

Allison, cocooned in the blankets, groaned from beneath her covers. "No, no, no... too early," she protested, her voice muffled and sleep-heavy.

As I glanced around the room, I noticed that most of the others were already out of their beds, some still squinting in the harsh light while others frantically searched their spaces. I knelt down and slid my hand under my mattress, feeling around in the dark crevice. Nothing. My heart sank a little, but I couldn't give up.

I pushed myself up and walked over to the makeup table, cluttered with various items that had been hastily tossed aside. As I began pushing things out of the way, my eye caught something taped to the back of a mirror. My pulse quickened with excitement as I grabbed the piece and shoved it into my pocket, a smile breaking across my face.

I darted across the room, scanning for any glimmer of the puzzle pieces we needed. The bright overhead lights made everything feel more frantic. I stumbled into Allison, her expression a mix of determination and annoyance as she rifled through her things.

"Have you found anything?" I asked, breathless.

"Nope," she shot back, her brows knitting together in concentration. "But I'm not leaving without at least one."

I nodded and turned away, my mind racing. Allison still lay buried under her blankets, but I couldn't afford to waste time on her right now. I made my way to the common area where the couches were strewn with cushions, all haphazardly tossed aside during our frantic wake-up call.

I flipped over a cushion. Nothing. I shoved another aside, feeling a bit like a detective on a wild goose chase. Each second ticked away as the countdown loomed in my mind.

"Jessica!" Carolynn voice broke through my thoughts. "Look over here!"

I hurried back to her side just in time to see her hold up a piece with a flourish—a vibrant splash of color that hinted at a larger picture yet to be revealed.

"Nice find!" I exclaimed, feeling a flicker of hope igniting within me.

"Let's keep moving," she said, urgency creeping into her tone.

We split up again, my feet pounding against the floor as I darted from room to room. In the kitchen, I pried open cabinets and rummaged through drawers filled with mismatched utensils. The clattering echoed in my ears, each sound a reminder of how little time we had left.

A sudden flash of something shiny caught my eye near the back of the top shelf. Stretching on tiptoe, I barely managed to snag it—another piece! The bright colors sparkled under the fluorescent lights as I added it to my pocket.

"You're killing it!" Carolynn cheered from behind me, making me spin around with newfound energy.

"I'm not done yet," I shot back playfully before bolting toward the hallway leading to our shared rooms again.

Suddenly, Leslie burst into the kitchen, hair tousled and eyes wide with determination. "I found one!

Look!" She held out her hand triumphantly.

"Great! We're getting closer," I encouraged her as we shared a quick grin before diving back into our frantic search once more.

Time slipped away like sand through our fingers as we combed through every corner we could reach— the walls felt closer than ever before.

Determined, I continued my search around the center, looking under chairs and tables, peering into the fridge and stove, flipping up pillows to examine what lay beneath them. I had collected five pieces when the alarm blared once more. "Place your puzzle pieces on the top of your locker and return to your beds. All puzzle pieces have been found."

"Well, that was interesting," Dot broke the silence, her voice cutting through the tension.

Leslie chimed in, sounding a bit defeated. "I don't think I did well; I only got four."

As I walked back to my bed, I elbowed Carolynn playfully and whispered, "I got five. You?"

"Three," she shrugged, a hint of disappointment creeping into her tone. "The boys seemed to be doing pretty good, though."

I turned my gaze over to the group of boys in the corner, who were high-fiving each other with apparent excitement. I realized I hadn't even spoken to any of them yet, and a wave of unease washed over me. This could be bad for me.

"I don't think Gemma even woke up," Allison announced with a laugh, her words punctuated by a hint of disbelief.

I hadn't spoken much with Gemma and hadn't even realized she wasn't running around with us. I tried to recall what she had said at dinner last night. She seemed so simple and quiet, lost in her own world. Clearly, she was also very tired, perhaps even more than any of us.

Climbing back into my bed, I felt the weight of exhaustion creeping in again and decided to send a quick text to Mia and Grace:

Jessica: "First competition complete!"

Grace: "You've got this!"

With a soft sigh, I buried my face in my pillow, letting the world fade away as I drifted off into a much- needed sleep.

∞∞∞∞∞

Several hours later, I stirred awake in a tranquil bedroom, the soft light filtering through the curtains casting a gentle glow. Carolynn, Allison, and a few others were still deep in slumber, their rhythmic breathing filling the room with a peaceful ambiance. I could hear some voices drifting in from the kitchen, chatting softly, the sound a warm invitation to the day ahead.

I crept over to my locker, the familiar metallic clink echoing in the stillness as I managed to pry it open. Inside, a few outfits hung neatly, each one a potential choice for the day. I contemplated my options carefully, not wanting to come across as overly eager but still hoping to catch the attention of the house hunters and observers who would be watching our every move. After a moment's consideration, I opted for a knee-length pink sundress that felt light and breezy, paired with simple white sneakers that would keep me comfortable. I felt cute enough without being too flashy, which was exactly the balance I was aiming for.

Settling down at the makeup table, I straightened my hair, fingers deftly working to smooth out the tangles. I applied some simple makeup, just enough to enhance my features without masking who I truly was. After a final glance in the mirror, I decided I was ready and made my way to the kitchen, butterflies of anticipation fluttering in my stomach.

"Hey, Jess. Good morning. Want some coffee?" Dot greeted me cheerfully, her bright smile infectious.

I nodded, grateful for the caffeine fix, and joined her at the breakfast bar where Leslie sat, her nose buried in a book. Dot went over to the coffee maker, where Shane, the guy who had defended her the previous night, stood pouring himself a cup. I could see the camaraderie between them, a bond formed over shared experiences.

I turned my attention to Carolynn, who was busy arranging a plate of pastries. "So... what's next?" I asked, curiosity lacing my voice.

"Probably an announcement of the winner," another one of the guys interjected while handing me a cup of coffee, his name eluding me for the moment—I think it was Mike.

As if someone had heard our conversation and decided to make it official, an announcement blared over the loudspeaker, startling us all. "We have a winner. Shane, please report to the office for questioning."

Shane's face lit up with excitement, his eyes wide as he processed the news. "Oh wow, guys!" He beamed, the joy radiating off him.

We all congratulated him as he made his way to the office, our cheers mingling in the air. However, the celebratory vibes were quickly drowned out by Allison, who was throwing a tantrum. "What? I thought you were going to win this, Eric!" she exclaimed, her voice a mix of disappointment and disbelief.

I hopped off my barstool, followed closely by Carolynn, intrigued by the commotion. We peeked into the bedroom to find Allison playfully straddling Eric in his bed, hitting him lightly as if to emphasize her frustration. I couldn't help but chuckle at the sight, returning to my coffee as I grabbed a book from a nearby shelf. I made myself comfortable on the couch, opening the pages and losing myself in a tale about a werewolf king, the world around me fading away as I delved into the story

Chapter 3

Jessica

Everyone, head to the backyard right away," the loudspeaker's message boomed through the air, cutting through the chatter and laughter that had filled the room just moments before. Instinctively, we all hurried to comply, a mix of confusion and urgency propelling us forward.

As we made our way outside, the brief pause that followed was punctuated by awkward sexual jokes exchanged between Eric and Allison, their laughter ringing out like a desperate attempt to lighten the mood. It felt out of place, given the tension that hung over us like a storm cloud. Just then, Shane appeared, his expression serious as he clutched an envelope in his hand.

"I'm sorry, everyone," he said, his voice steady but laced with an undercurrent of tension as he cleared his throat, the sound echoing in the heavy silence that enveloped us. "I had to rank all of you. The two at the bottom are at risk of being eliminated." As he nervously opened the envelope, the air grew thick with apprehension, each heartbeat amplifying the anxiety that crackled around us like static electricity. "I truly regret this. Gemma and Mike, you are the bottom two."

I felt my heart sink, an icy weight settling in my stomach as I took a seat beside Dot. She immediately reached out, her fingers wrapping around Shane's hand in an instinctive attempt to offer him some comfort. His expression was somber, a mixture of concern and determination etched into his features, and I could sense the weight of his words pressing down on him like a physical burden.

"It's fine," Gemma broke the tense quiet, her voice surprisingly steady, though I could hear the faint tremor beneath it. "I didn't even participate in the competition." There was a hint of defiance in her tone, yet it was overshadowed by the resignation I saw in her eyes, a flicker of acceptance that made my heart ache for her. In that moment, I wished I could sweep away the reality of our situation, to take us all far from this place where our worth was measured and our lives dictated by the whims of others.

Mike, a guy I hadn't had the chance to speak with, remained silent, sulking in the corner like a shadow retreating from the light. His expression was clouded, and I could see the tension in his shoulders as he hunched over, almost as if he were trying to disappear entirely. The news had clearly hit him hard, and I felt a pang of sympathy for him. It was a familiar feeling—this weight of despair that seemed to hang in the air, heavy and suffocating. I wished I could reach out, break through his silence, but I didn't know what to say. Instead, I watched him withdraw further into himself, and it made my heart ache for all of us caught in this tangled web of expectations and disappointments.

Suddenly, a man dressed in a suit stepped out of the house, his presence commanding and intimidating. "Hello," he said in a stern tone that sent a chill through the group. His gaze was intense, and it felt like he could see right through us. The suit he wore seemed more expensive than what my entire family earned in a year. "I am Mr. Jones. I will serve as your Center Liaison, delivering special messages from the House Hunters and the viewers."

"What?" Allison interjected, confusion and defiance etched across her face, her voice sharper than I'd ever heard. "I've never heard of this happening before."

With a predatory grace, Mr. Jones moved closer to her, the tension in the air thickening as he reached around and yanked her hair back forcefully. Her cry of shock and pain pierced through the uneasy silence, sending a shiver down my spine. "You do not question the system, you ungrateful brat," he hissed, his voice low and dripping with venom, each word laced with menace.

After a moment that felt like an eternity, he released her hair and returned to the front of the group, his demeanor chillingly calm, as if he had merely adjusted a tie rather than inflicted pain. "As I call out these names, you will line up against the wall," he began, his tone authoritative and cold, and we exchanged anxious glances, each of us bracing for what was to come. "Allison, Paige, Leslie, Dottie, Malorie, and Jerry. Please face the wall."

The six of them quickly lined up as instructed, their expressions a mixture of anger and fear. Allison and Paige appeared furious, their resentment practically radiating off them like heat from a fire, while the others looked apprehensive, their eyes wide as the grim reality of the situation settled in, heavy and suffocating. I felt a knot tighten in my stomach, the dread pooling inside me as I watched my friends confront the nightmare that had just begun.

Mr. Jones reached into a case resting against the wall, retrieving six bracelets, each one glinting ominously in the sunlight. He tightly fastened one around each of their wrists, the click of the clasps echoing in the tense atmosphere. "The House Hunters and viewers are displeased with you. It could be your attitude, your looks, or simply your submitted profile. Regardless, you have garnered the least interest, which is unacceptable for our community." Hearing him speak about people with such disdain was painful, a harsh reminder of the stakes we all faced.

"You will learn respect," he spat, his glare landing squarely on Allison and Paige. A shiver of fear coursed down my spine, the malice in his eyes chilling me to the core as if his contempt were a tangible force. I could feel my heart racing, the pit of my stomach tightening at the thought of what he might do next.

His attention shifted to Leslie and Dot, and I could see the tension in their shoulders, the way they instinctively recoiled as if bracing for a blow. "You will understand the importance of putting effort into your appearance," he said, his voice dripping with disdain, each word laced with a cruel reminder of the superficial expectations we were forced to endure. I felt a surge of anger for my friends, and I silently wished I could shield them from his venomous words.

"And you both need to work on being less forgettable," he snapped at Malorie and Jerry, his words cutting through the air like daggers aimed directly at their already fragile self-esteem. I could feel the weight of his judgment pressing down on us, a suffocating reminder of how easily our worth could be dismissed in this cruel game.

"These bracelets will shock you if you eat," Mr. Jones sneered, the cruelty in his voice unmistakable as he turned on his heel, striding back towards the door with a confidence that made my stomach churn. "I'll return tomorrow, so don't worry.

His words hung in the air, a sinister promise that twisted like a knife in my gut.

And just like that, he was gone, the heavy door slamming shut behind him, leaving a silence that felt more suffocating than any of the dread we'd been carrying. It was a silence thick with unspoken fears, the collective anxiety of my friends palpable in the stillness. I could feel the tension crackling around us, each heartbeat echoing the unrelenting reality of our situation.

The afternoon felt like a haze, as if I were moving through a dream laced with uncertainty. There were many tears shed over the bracelets today, each drop a symbol of our collective anxiety, and I found myself incessantly pestering Shane about how he evaluated everyone else in the house. His insights had become a lifeline for me, a way to navigate the shifting dynamics that felt so overwhelming.

Around 4 pm, a sudden announcement pierced through the fog, declaring that certain individuals were required to participate in a lock-breaking contest. My heart raced at the thought of being chosen, but fortunately, I wasn't picked. Leslie, with her quiet determination, ended up winning the contest. After a visit to the office, she returned to us without her hunger bracelet, a small victory that brought a wave of relief over our group. We were all grateful for this reward as she enthusiastically offered to prepare dinner, her smile a beacon of normalcy amidst the chaos.

However, dinner turned out to be more uncomfortable than anyone could have anticipated. With seven of us at the table, the atmosphere felt strained, while the others chose to stay locked away in the bedroom, avoiding the scene altogether. Allison had thrown a fit, insisting that Eric should choose not to eat, her emotions spilling over in a way that made the rest of us uneasy. In the end, though, Eric surprisingly joined us in the kitchen, his presence both a comfort and a reminder of what we were all fighting against.

Right after dinner, the loudspeaker crackled to life, summoning us one by one into the office for debriefs. I felt a flutter of anxiety in my stomach as my name echoed through the space.

"Jessica," the call was straightforward yet impactful, slicing through the tension in the air.

I stepped inside to find Camilla seated at a desk, her auburn hair neatly pulled back, a picture of polished authority. "Hi, dear, please have a seat," she welcomed me with a warmth that was both comforting and disarming. "Are you alright?"

I nodded, still surprised to see her there, her presence somehow grounding me amidst the whirlwind of emotions. "Are you handling all my debriefs?" I slumped into the chair, feeling the weight of the day pressing down on me.

"Of course. Did you think you could manage this on your own?" She chuckled lightly, the sound a blend of amusement and genuine concern. "Remember your manners, Jessica. They like you, but you're not the favorite. You need some tact."

Her words struck a chord, making me realize I hadn't truly considered the various elements that would require me to adjust my strategy as we progressed. "Thank you, Camilla," I nodded, the sincerity of my gratitude surprising even myself. It was the first time I had expressed appreciation to her, and I recognized that she had been genuinely assisting me in navigating this treacherous landscape.

Her smile lit up the office like a ray of sunshine. "That wasn't so hard, was it?" she giggled, her laughter easing some of my tension. "Now, let's get down to business. Who do you think is least deserving of staying in the competition?"

"Wait," I was taken aback. "I get to decide who stays?"

She shook her head, her expression shifting to one of seriousness. "Not just you; all of you will decide." She gestured toward the door, her tone grave. "But it's against the rules to discuss it with anyone else in there."

"Gemma," I blurted out, the name escaping my lips before I could reconsider.

Camilla's smile reemerged, bright and approving, illuminating her previously serious demeanor. "Exactly what I was thinking, good girl," she said, her voice warm and encouraging. I felt a rush of relief at her validation. With a swift motion, she typed my answer into the computer, her fingers dancing across the keys with practiced ease. "Now off you go," she instructed, gesturing toward the door as if ushering me into a new chapter of this bizarre competition. I took a deep breath, ready to face whatever awaited me beyond that threshold.

As I left, the loudspeaker summoned us all to the living room, and I felt a wave of dread wash over me. Mr. Jones was waiting near the fireplace, his presence commanding and intimidating.

"Let's make this quick. Unlike you, I have appointments to keep and places to go." He chuckled darkly, the sound sending chills down myspine. "Gemma, someone will be by to collect your belongings. Your time in the center is over. Based on what I've seen, you'll probably be spending it lying on your back somewhere since you're best in bed."

Gemma broke down in tears at his cruel words, her despair palpable as Mr. Jones approached her with an unsettling confidence. "Bye, guys," she sniffled, her voice trembling as she waved goodbye, the gesture feeling like a desperate farewell, as if she were being taken away from us for good and we might never see her again.

With a swift and almost dismissive motion, he escorted her out the door, the sound of it closing echoing in my ears like a death knell. Almost immediately, a young man in coveralls appeared, his expression blank as he began to gather her things, efficiently packing up the remnants of her presence. The finality of it all settled heavily in the air, a weight that pressed down on my chest and made it difficult to breathe. I couldn't shake the feeling that this was just the beginning of something far more sinister.

We all retreated to our beds, the oppressive silence broken only by the sound of rumbling stomachs echoing in the room. I couldn't help but notice that Allison and Eric were sharing a bed, their connection a stark contrast to the tension surrounding the rest of us.

Feeling restless, I grabbed my phone and quickly texted Grace and Mia, hoping for some sense of normalcy amidst the chaos:

Jessica: Where's my knight?

Mia: That bad?

Grace: You're brilliant; you can handle this.

Their words offered a small comfort, a reminder that I wasn't alone in this battle.

Chapter 4

Jessica

"CAROLYNN, PLEASE REPORT TO THE YARD."

The loudspeaker jolted me from my sound sleep, its piercing tone cutting through the hazy remnants of my dreams like a knife. I blinked against the harsh fluorescent light filtering through the thin curtains, struggling to shake off the lingering fog of slumber. Stretching my limbs, I felt the stiffness of sleep dissipate, but not before I turned to glance at my phone: 7 AM. Great—clearly, the folks running this place had zero appreciation for the concept of sleeping in. I sighed, a mix of annoyance and resignation bubbling up within me.

With a heavy heart, I swung my legs over the edge of my bed and padded my way to the shower, the cool tiles sending a shiver up my spine. The water was refreshing against my skin, a brief escape from the sterile atmosphere that enveloped this place. As I lathered my hair with fragrant shampoo, I began to think about the day ahead, filled with a sense of dread that seemed to grow heavier with each passing moment. The announcement blared again; thankfully, they called for Allison this time. I couldn't help but chuckle to myself—serves her right for staying up all night goofing off with Eric, her charming distraction who was always just a little too handsome for his own good.

I wondered if she had any idea how lucky she was to have someone like him. A part of me envied their carefree moments, laughing and flirting in a world that felt increasingly gray and lifeless. I rinsed the shampoo from my hair, the scent of coconut and vanilla swirling around me for just a fleeting moment, reminding me of the simpler times before Center 2742 had hijacked our lives. As I stepped out of the shower, I couldn't shake the feeling that every day spent here was another day stripped of our individuality, a relentless routine that threatened to dull the vibrant colors of our youth. I shampooed and conditioned my hair, my mind still wandering, as I prepared to face whatever awaited me in the yard.

I hurriedly rinsed off, finished my shower, and dashed to my locker. I slipped into a pair of black leggings that hugged my curves, a red sports bra that contrasted boldly against my pale skin, and a black crop top that showed just a hint of midriff. After pulling my long blonde hair into a high ponytail, I approached the makeup table, glancing in the mirror at my reflection. It was clear the watchers would be observing closely today, so I opted for some dark eyeshadow and bold mascara, hoping to draw attention away from any flaws. After the negative feedback the group received yesterday, I wanted to steer clear of any trouble myself.

"Well, look at you, little vixen," Paige whispered as she crept up behind me, her perfectly straight hair swinging as she leaned in closer. "You really can't think you have a chance at winning this, can you? You're clearly not wife material." Her words landed like a weight in my stomach, heavy and unwelcome.

I turned to meet her gaze, forcing my voice to remain steady despite the sting of her remarks. "You must be speaking out of hunger; I'm truly sorry," I replied, giving her my sweetest fake smile that I could muster, one that didn't quite reach my eyes. The weight of her words hung in the air between us, but I refused to let them settle in my heart. I slipped on my sandals, feeling the coolness of the floor beneath my feet, and made my way to the kitchen, determined not to let her get under my skin.

As I entered the kitchen, I took a deep breath, letting the familiar scents envelop me. I began to prepare an omelet, the rhythmic motions calming me as I cracked the eggs, their shells breaking with a satisfying sound, and whisked them together with a practiced ease. Each movement felt like a small act of defiance, a reminder that I could create something nourishing and beautiful, even amid the swirling chaos of my surroundings. Just as I was about to add the cheese, savoring the thought of its creamy richness melting into the egg, Allison came back from the yard, a look of faux innocence plastered on her face that made my stomach churn. Almost immediately, the announcement rang out, echoing through the house: "JESSICA, PLEASE REPORT TO THE YARD."

Upon my arrival, I was greeted by an intimidating pile of wood and an instruction sheet that read, "For some suitors, the ideal spouse will be handy. Today you are to build a functional piece of wooden furniture in 15 minutes. The best piece will be the winner and complete today's ranking." My heart raced as I took in the challenge ahead of me.

I quickly assessed my materials, my mind racing with a whirlwind of ideas. The pressure of the tight time limit bore down on me, and I decided to construct something relatively small yet sturdy. Having grown up with a father who was a skilled furniture builder, I had absorbed a fair amount of knowledge along the way. I wanted my creation to represent me proudly, a testament to my upbringing and the bond we shared. After a moment of contemplation, I settled on making a toy box—a simple yet meaningful project that held a certain nostalgia for me.

With determination, I grabbed the wood, hammer, nails, tape measure, and level, each item feeling familiar in my hands. As I leveled the sides and hammered the pieces together, my thoughts drifted back to the joyful times spent building with my dad as a child. I could almost hear his laughter echoing in my ears as we worked side by side in our garage, surrounded by the scent of sawdust and the warmth of the afternoon sun streaming through the open door.

"Five minutes remaining," the announcement cut through my daydream, snapping me back to the present with a jolt. My heart raced as I glanced at the toy box, nearly finished but still requiring my full attention. I quickly attached hinges to the top and handles to the sides, my pulse pounding with anticipation and a hint of anxiety. Would it be good enough? Would it stand out among the others? The stakes felt higher than ever as I pushed myself to complete my creation in time.

Before I realized it, the announcement rang out loud and clear: "Time is up." A wave of disbelief washed over me as I stepped back to admire my work, the culmination of all my effort and creativity. A smile broke across my face, stretching from ear to ear; it looked fantastic, a perfect blend of my childhood memories and my hopes for the future. Each detail seemed to reflect a piece of me—every curve and color whispered stories of laughter and dreams, a tangible representation of the journey I had taken. In that moment, I felt a swell of pride, knowing I had poured my heart into this creation.

It had been a lengthy day, filled with the weight of everyone tackling their individual challenges and the emotional toll that came with it. Dot was the final participant, wrapping up her session shortly after one o'clock in the afternoon, her relief palpable as she stepped away from the spotlight, a small smile breaking through her usual reserved demeanor.

We gathered around the breakfast bar, the atmosphere buzzing with a low hum of quiet conversation that floated like a comforting blanket enveloping us in a momentary reprieve from our worries. As we talked about our homes, the conversation gradually shifted to the topic of pets, a subject that seemed to ignite a spark in everyone, breathing life into our otherwise heavy hearts. It became abundantly clear that Carolynn had a number of animals since she lived on a farm, a fact that seemed to bring her some warmth as she animatedly spoke of her furry companions. Dot shared her fond memories of the two lovebirds she clearly missed deeply, her eyes lighting up with each word, a mix of nostalgia and longing in her voice.

Meanwhile, some of the guys chimed in, sharing stories about their dogs, their faces glowing with affection, laughter erupting like the joyful barks of a beloved pet.

I remained mostly silent during this exchange, feeling a familiar pang of longing gnawing at me. Although I had always yearned for a dog, my household had never embraced the idea of pets. My mom would often remind us, "It's just one more thing that would be taken from you when you have to leave." I could still hear my siblings' complaints echoing in my mind, their voices tinged with frustration and sadness about how unfair it was that we couldn't have pets just because Mom was worried about me. I found myself wondering how long it would be after I left before my brother finally got a pet of his own, a small part of me hoping he wouldn't have to wait too long to experience that joy.

Suddenly, I snapped back to the conversation when I sensed an awkward silence enveloping most of the group, like a thick fog settling over us. I caught Allison calling herself a "pussy cat," her playful tone ringing in the air, and Eric jokingly claimed that she was the only one for him, his voice lighthearted yet slightly too loud in the charged atmosphere. Did they not realize they were surrounded by nine other people, with who knows how many more eyes watching us from the shadows, weighing our every word and action?

"JERRY, YOU HAVE WON THE WOODWORKING COMPETITION. PLEASE REPORT TO THE OFFICE FOR RANKING," a voice announced, cutting through the tension like a knife.

Jerry was a reserved guy; this afternoon was really the only time I had heard him speak beyond his nondescript introduction, and that was solely about his dog. He stood around six feet tall, his dark eyes and hair contrasting with his fit physique, a quiet yet undeniably attractive presence. He possessed a skill with tools that would certainly make him appealing to women in search of a husband, even if he seemed completely unaware of that fact.

He stood up silently, like a shadow slipping away, and made his way to the office, avoiding eye contact with anyone as though the weight of our gazes was too much to bear. Once the door clicked shut behind him, Carolynn got up and headed toward the bedroom, gesturing for me to follow her with a subtle nod.

The others seemed completely oblivious to our exit, lost in their animated discussion about their latest creations, their laughter mingling with the air like a carefree melody that felt foreign to my ears.

Carolynn plopped down onto my bed, and I followed suit, sinking into the familiar comfort of my space, where the soft sheets and the faint scent of lavender instantly put me at ease, wrapping me in a sense of security I desperately craved.

She shook her head, her expression a mix of frustration and uncertainty that tugged at my heart. "I've hardly spoken to him; I have no clue how he will rank me," she whispered, her voice barely above a murmur, as if the weight of her worries could somehow be lessened by keeping them between us.

It dawned on me then that I hadn't been considering that aspect at all. "Oh no, I haven't said two words to him either. At least you and Leslie cook for us!

Nobody wants the cooks to leave," I reassured her, hoping to lift her spirits and distract her from her anxious thoughts.

Carolynn nodded, her shoulders easing slightly as she absorbed my words, a flicker of hope appearing in her eyes. "You're good people, Jessica. You know that, right? You're not playing a flirtation game or pushing your story or trying to sell your skills like the rest of us. You're just being yourself. I want you to know that I recognize your honesty, and I value it," she said earnestly, her gaze steady and sincere.

I shook my head, astonished by the idea that I seemed to be sailing through a game I hadn't realized others were participating in. "You're not doing any of those things either," I countered, feeling a rush of solidarity wash over me.

Carolynn burst into a hearty laugh, her joy infectious and brightening the dim room. "I don't cook for you all just because I like you. I'm aiming to be the cook for my assignment, you idiot," she playfully smacked my arm, her warmth enveloping me like a cozy blanket. "Haven't you figured out what you really want, Jessica?"

"I just want to be myself," I shrugged, instantly aware that it was the most foolish answer I could give. I understood how these centers operated all too well. I knew I'd have a job after this, but I sounded like a child, somehow clinging to the naïve hope that someone watching would offer me a job simply for being me. "Is there a job for going to the movies and eating ice cream with my friends? Because I would really love that one," I giggled, tears welling in my eyes as the absurdity of it all swept over me like a wave, crashing against the shore of my reality.

Chapter 5

Connor

Her voice was gentle, pure, and soothing, wrapping around me like a warm blanket. "I just want to be myself," she confided sincerely to her companion, her words echoing in my mind long after they left her lips.

I focused intently on the monitor at my desk, my eyes glued to the stream of Center 2742. For the past 36 hours, I'd barely glanced away, except during the moments when she slept. I rested while she rested, trusting my assistant Jonathan to keep a watchful eye on the stream, rousing me whenever she stirred. Jonathan was more than just a worker; he was my first and only employee, someone I had chosen from the center six months ago when I celebrated my 20th birthday. He was intelligent, clever, and compassionate, embodying qualities that made him more of a friend than mere staff, or a servant as the government liked to label him. Despite the constant pressure I faced to "fill my house," I knew I had to hold off for her, for Jessica.

Jess was more stunning and compassionate than I could have ever envisioned, a radiant light in a world shrouded in darkness. Her presence had a way of illuminating even the gloomiest of days, and it was impossible not to be drawn to her warmth. My uncle had quietly discussed her with me since my childhood, weaving her story into the fabric of my own life like a gentle thread that bound us together. She was the niece of his first wife, Clara, who had tragically died in a horrific car accident that left a void not only in Uncle Roger's heart but in the lives of those who loved her. Uncle Roger had genuinely adored Clara, even if their initial meeting had been through the centers—an ironic twist of fate that made their love story all the more poignant. He had vowed to do everything he could to ensure Jess would have a good life, far removed from the homes filled with corporal punishment and narcissistic heads of households, which seemed to be the norm in our society.

Unfortunately, Uncle Roger's second wife from the centers, Tess, embodied everything he despised, a constant reminder of the chains that bound so many like us. To protect Jess from that fate, he kept tabs on her himself, gathering every scrap of information he could without arousing suspicion. This was a secret known only to me, a sacred bond between us that I cherished deeply.

It felt like a hidden alliance against a world that sought to control us, a promise that we would fight for her future together.

We would take monthly retreats to a secluded cabin in the woods, a sanctuary where we could fish and escape the harsh realities of our lives, if only for a little while. During those trips, Uncle Roger would share his dreams, painting a vivid picture of how he wished he could have run his household, a vision filled with love, respect, and understanding. He spoke fondly of Clara, recounting stories of their hidden aspirations to live free from the constraints of the centers. Each tale he spun inspired me, instilling a sense of purpose within me that I had never felt before. He motivated me and taught me how to be a "good husband" when I grew up, filling my head with tales of life before the centers existed—a topic strictly forbidden in our society, but one that ignited a fire within me, pushing me to dream of a better tomorrow.

Around the age of ten, I recall a teacher saying, "If you want to improve this country, everyone must know your name." That moment solidified my resolve to make a difference in the world, however possible. The teacher likely meant "for better," suggesting widening the gap between the powerful and the impoverished, but I interpreted her advice differently. I wanted to bridge that gap, to create a world where compassion outweighed greed, where love and kindness could flourish in a society that often seemed intent on snuffing them out.

I took control of my first factory two years ago, right after I became a legal adult at 18. Driven by ambition, I expanded it into a million-dollar enterprise. It collaborated with small family businesses, offering their products to a larger audience of buyers instead of limiting them to local customers. Dandin Enterprises became a familiar name, a beacon of hope where most people conducted their online shopping. It elevated my name, Connor Dandin, to a household level, a stepping stone in my quest for change.

"Hey Connor," Jonathan nudged me in the side, pulling me back from my reverie. "Did you catch that?"

"What?" I realized I'd completely missed the moment. Looking at the screen, Jessica appeared just as stunned as I was, her expression mirroring my own.

"She was ranked lowest. Sorry, man. Do you want me to send the request to have her assigned here if she's booted tonight? You just need to sign this form." He slid a paper toward me, the weight of decision heavy in the air.

I shook my head, resolute in my choice. "No. Do what needs to be done; she should be reassigned to a new center." My hands rifled through a folder of documents, my heart racing as I located the ones for Center #3303 and #1410. "One of these will do. I'll pay any sum necessary. Make it happen."

My office felt like a shell, a space stripped of character. The walls wore a dull grey, devoid of any artwork or personal touches. A single potted plant sat in the corner, its leaves wilting from neglect. I'd been too busy to think about decor, too focused on the demands of running my company and figuring out how to save Jessica from her fate. A large mahogany desk dominated the room, cluttered with reports and documents that screamed for attention but went mostly ignored.

Jonathan shifted his weight beside me, his brows furrowed in concern. "You should really consider adding some life to this place," he remarked, his eyes sweeping over the barren space.

"Yeah, well, I haven't exactly had time to redecorate." I leaned back in my chair, letting the leather creak under my weight as I rubbed my temples. The starkness of the room mirrored my state of mind— chaotic yet empty, filled with tasks but lacking inspiration.

The floor beneath me was polished concrete, cool against my bare feet as I shifted positions. My gaze fell upon the window—large and unobstructed— offering a panoramic view of the city skyline. It should have been inspiring; instead, it felt like a reminder of everything I was fighting against—a constant barrage of wealth and privilege just beyond reach.

"Seriously," Jonathan pressed on, "we could make this place feel more like home. It wouldn't hurt." He had a point. A couple of framed photographs or some vibrant paintings might lighten the oppressive atmosphere.

I chuckled softly, imagining my office decorated with colorful artwork or quirky sculptures. "You think some flowers will change anything? They won't solve our problems."

"No," he admitted with a shrug. "But they might remind you

that there's still hope out there."

He stepped back to study me for a moment before moving toward the window. "I can handle getting some pieces for you if you want," he offered casually.

I waved him off, lost in thought about Jessica and her struggles within those cold walls at the center. "Just focus on getting her moved to the holding facility if things go south."

Jonathan nodded but lingered near the window, taking in the view while I sat surrounded by emptiness that mirrored my own fears for Jessica's future—a stark contrast to what she deserved.

He stared at the papers, a mixture of surprise and curiosity in his eyes. "Does this mean you're going to have a wife? I know I'm good, but you don't even have a full team of staff. I'm not sure any woman would be satisfied with our grilled cheese sandwiches and takeout for dinner every night."

"She's precisely who we need." I couldn't suppress the smile that crept onto my face. "But get me the papers to request Carolynn on my staff once she gets booted."

Jonathan perked up immediately, his eyes lighting up with enthusiasm. I had noticed the interest he had shown in Carolynn while watching the stream earlier; it was hard to miss the way he leaned in whenever she spoke, a subtle admiration in his gaze. He clearly had a crush. "Got it, boss. She's cute too!" he said, a playful wink accompanying his words. With that, he made his way to the door, energy radiating from him like a burst of sunlight, and I couldn't help but smile at the infectious excitement he carried.

I quickly called out, my voice rising slightly to cut through the excitement in the air, "And I want that toy box Jess built while you're at it. Don't forget!" The thought of that beautifully crafted piece, a testament to her talent, brought a smile to my face. It was the kind of personal touch that could brighten any room and remind me of the warmth she would bring to this home.

Staring at the screen, I longed to reach out and embrace her, to bridge the distance that separated us. We hadn't even met yet, but I knew I would move mountains for her. She just needed to stay strong in the centers and succeed for me, and I would do everything in my power to make that happen.

Chapter 6

Jessica

I remained in the living room, completely taken aback by the sudden shift in our dynamic. My gaze instinctively shot daggers at Jerry, my heart pounding in my chest as the realization sunk in that I had found myself among the bottom two.

"I'm sorry, Jessica and Paige. It's nothing personal; I just did what had to be done." His voice was devoid of any real emotion as he stood up and trudged toward the bedroom, leaving a heavy silence in his wake.

Paige was seething, her anger palpable. "What the hell?" she exclaimed, her voice echoing through the room as she stormed outside, with Allison and Eric trailing her like shadows, each of them caught up in their own whirlwind of emotions.

The others scattered to various rooms, their footsteps echoing the mix of shock and uncertainty that gripped us all. It felt as if the very air had thickened with tension, leaving Carolynn, Shane, Leslie, and me on the couches, each of us wrestling with the heavy fallout of the voting. I could sense the weight of their thoughts swirling around us, unsaid words hanging in the air like a storm waiting to break.

"I'm sorry, Jessica," Shane was the first to speak, his voice low and sincere. He and the others weren't allowed to discuss their votes, but the weight of his tone conveyed more than mere words could express. It was a mix of regret and sympathy that made my heart ache.

Leslie, always the peacemaker, tried to shift the conversation. "I wonder when they'll let everyone eat again. Paige and Allison are becoming quite unbearable to deal with," she observed, attempting to lighten the mood with a hint of humor.

"That's putting it mildly," Carolynn added with a small, wry smile, but it did little to ease the tension that hung in the air.

As if he had been listening from afar, Mr. Jones walked in through the front door, his presence immediately commanding attention. He positioned himself in front of the kitchen table, a dark cloud looming over us.

"EVERYONE TO THE KITCHEN!" The announcement blared over the loudspeakers, shaking me from my thoughts. We quickly gathered, the urgency of his command pushing us into action. Paige and I were instructed to sit next to each other, as the two lowest scorers, with Jerry seated across from us as the daily winner, wearing that smug expression that made my skin crawl.

"Allison, Paige, Malorie, Dot, and Jerry, please join me," he said flatly, turning his focus to them once they had assembled. "I trust you've learned your lesson." The way he said it sent chills down my spine.

They quickly responded in unison, their voices ringing out as they agreed they had learned, expressing their hunger, and promising to do better. Mr. Jones removed the bracelets from their wrists, locking them away in a box that he placed in the center of the kitchen table, a stark reminder of their failure.

"The bracelets will remain here as a reminder that you all must be on your best behavior." His smile was anything but warm. "Every government post and home you will be assigned to will have these same bracelets at their disposal; many already possess them. Should you forget your place, overindulge, or underperform, they are just one of many tools available to remind you of your duty and purpose on this earth." His words dripped with a sinister undertone that made my stomach churn.

Paige's stomach growled loudly, a sound that cut through the tension, interrupting his speech. "Guess I better behave," she muttered under her breath, but I could see the fear in her eyes.

Before any of us could react, Mr. Jones pulled a small whip from his pocket, a cruel glint in his eye, and struck Paige across the hand with a swift motion, making her scream in pain—a sound that echoed in my ears and sent a jolt of panic through my veins.

"Stop." My instincts kicked in, and I instinctively grasped her hand, trying to shield Paige from another lash, desperate to protect her from further harm.

Instantly, I regretted my action as I felt the whip come down across my back, then my arm—a sharp, searing pain that sent shockwaves through my body. "If you want to be foolish enough to take someone else's punishment, be my guest, you foolish girl," Mr. Jones spat, his voice laced with contempt before delivering one last strike across my knuckles that left me gasping.

Before I could even process what had just occurred, he was gone, leaving behind a suffocating silence. I hunched over the table, tears streaming down my face from the pain, feeling the blood trickle down my back, a stark reminder of the brutality we endured. I shut my eyes tightly, wishing to be anywhere else but here, anywhere away from the torment.

In moments, I heard Shane's voice, a lifeline in my sea of despair. "This is going to sting, but please try not to move." I sensed the familiar sting of antiseptic on my back, followed by the gentle application of bandages, his touch both comforting and painful.

"Thank you," I managed to whisper through the agony, my voice barely a breath.

"Don't thank me yet; we still have your arm and hand to tend to," he said kindly, his demeanor calm and reassuring as he addressed the other injuries, helping me to bed, a silent guardian in the storm.

∞∞∞∞∞

"JESSICA, PAIGE, AND SHANE PLEASE REPORT TO THE YARD." The announcement jolted me awake, pulling me from a restless slumber filled with anxious thoughts.

Carolynn hurried over to assist me in getting ready, her presence a comforting balm against the rising tide of my nerves. She helped me adjust my clothes, giving a reassuring smile as we made our way to the door. "Good luck, you've got this," she said softly, her words wrapping around me like a warm embrace as I stepped outside into the harsh reality of our situation.

As I crossed the threshold, I spotted Shane and Paige standing at tables, their expressions a mixture of apprehension and determination. Mr. Jones loomed ominously in front of them, a figure we all knew too well. I quickly took my place at a third table, my gaze falling on the electrical board laid out before me, a jumbled mess of wires and bulbs.

"Thank you all for gathering so promptly," Mr. Jones began, his tone slick with condescension as he completely overlooked the fact that just hours earlier he had publicly punished two of us with no remorse. "Jessica and Paige, you have the opportunity to save yourselves today. However, if one of you wins, Shane will take your spot. Thus, we deemed it fair to give Shane a chance to save himself as well, allowing him to compete alongside you. If Shane emerges victorious, either Jessica or Paige will be leaving the center tonight."

My heart raced as we exchanged shocked glances. Competitions like this were typically reserved for later in the cycle, and only when someone had been identified as a potential marriage candidate — a fate none of us wanted to contemplate.

As if sensing the dread thickening in the air, Mr. Jones continued, "Yes, this indicates that either Jessica or Paige has been identified as a potential for marriage already. I will not elaborate further on this matter," he huffed dismissively, waving a hand as though to brush aside our fears. "Before you lies a circuit; the first to complete it will win. The others will remain as the bottom two."

He nodded, a cruel smile creeping onto his face as he commenced a countdown. "Ready, set, go!"

I focused all my energy on finishing the circuit, desperately trying to recall what I had learned a few years back in basic electrical training. I recognized this could be a competition, but given that it wasn't a skill typically taught to girls like me, I hadn't devoted much time to mastering it. There were five small light bulbs and two batteries waiting for my attention. I began connecting wires as swiftly as my bandaged fingers could manage, heart pounding with each movement. After one bulb lit up, the sound of a buzzer echoed through the yard, indicating a winner.

Mr. Jones wore a smug expression that made my stomach churn. "Congratulations, Shane. You will all remain here, separated from the others, while they are called in for a debriefing. Shane, you will be the last to be called for debrief." He glanced at the three of us, his eyes cold. "I trust you know not to discuss what happens in the debrief if I leave you?" We all nodded quickly, the fear of his wrath hanging in the air like a thick fog, and he exited.

"CAROLYNN, PLEASE REPORT TO THE OFFICE FOR YOUR DEBRIEF." The announcement reverberated through the yard, and my heart sank further into my chest, a lead weight dragging me down. It was a stark reminder of our reality—a reality where people were called away like pawns on a chessboard, and I felt powerless to change it.

I enveloped Shane in a big hug, needing to feel the comforting warmth of friendship in such a cold, oppressive environment. "Congrats, Shane," I whispered, my voice barely above a murmur as I tried to convey my pride through the embrace.

"I'm sorry, Jessica. I could have lost, and maybe you would have won," he stammered, guilt etched across his face like a dark cloud threatening to burst. It pained me to see him like this, knowing he was wrestling with his own demons while trying to juggle the burden of our collective fate.

I shook my head, my voice firm and resolute. "No, you needed to win for yourself, Shane. I don't hold it against you. You really are good with wiring." My sincerity cut through the tension, and I hoped he could sense the truth in my words.

He smiled at me, a flicker of relief sparking in his eyes, but it was fleeting. Almost as if the weight of the situation had pressed down too hard for him to fully enjoy the moment. His gaze shifted to Paige, who stood nearby, visibly shaken.

"Sorry, Paige," he offered, his voice softening in her direction.

She looked up at him, tears brimming in her eyes, her voice trembling as she spoke. "I'm not the one who has a man out there waiting for me," she quivered, her vulnerability spilling forth like a cracked dam, exposing the rawness of her emotions. In that moment, I felt a pang of empathy for her; we were all fighting our own battles, and the stakes had never felt higher.

"I don't think it would be me," I retorted, shaking my head, feeling a swell of sympathy for her situation, even amidst my own turmoil.

We sat in silence for a few moments, the weight of our circumstances pressing down on us, until we heard Shane called to the office for his debrief. He quickly left, and I was left alone with Paige, the tension palpable between us.

"Thank you," she said, her voice barely above a whisper, a tremor of vulnerability threading through her words. "You didn't have to take those lashings for me." The weight of her gratitude hung in the air, heavy and poignant, and I could see the flicker of guilt in her eyes. It was as if she wished she could take back the pain I had endured on her behalf, though I knew deep down that I would do it again in a heartbeat if it meant shielding her from harm.

I shook my head vehemently. "You didn't deserve lashings for being hungry, and you shouldn't have been hungry because someone didn't like your behavior." The unfairness of it all ignited a fire in me, a desire to fight against the injustice we faced.

"I have a feeling I'll be hungry a lot after this," she laughed softly, a hint of defiance in her tone.

I smiled back at her, realizing for the first time that she might not be as annoying as I had once thought. "Not if you're in charge of the house and a wife," I joked, trying to lighten the mood.

"EVERYONE PLEASE REPORT TO THE LIVING ROOM IMMEDIATELY." The announcement was loud and clear, a grim reminder that either Paige or I would be leaving, never to see each other again.

We walked to the living room together, each step heavy with the uncertainty of what awaited us, taking our seats at the end of the couch as instructed by Mr. Jones. "Girls and boys, I am here once more to announce who will be leaving immediately. Their belongings will be retrieved for them, just like Gemma's."

He opened a small envelope in his hand, shaking his head as if the contents within were distasteful before reading it aloud. "The results were 6 to 3. Jessica, say goodbye. It's time to go."

I blinked rapidly, fighting back tears as I stood up, the reality of my situation crashing over me like a wave. "Bye, everyone. Good luck. Stay strong."

Unlike yesterday, everyone stood up after me, a show of solidarity I hadn't expected. Most came in for a hug, drawing me into a small cocoon of warmth and friendship.

"I'm sorry," Shane cried on my shoulder, his voice thick with emotion before Mr. Jones interrupted the farewells by opening the front door, signaling that I needed to leave.

I pulled away, only to be swiftly grabbed by Carolynn, who quickly enveloped me in a hug as I approached the door. "Don't give up," she whispered softly through my hair into my ear so no one else could hear. "You are going to change this world for all of us." Her words resonated deep within me, a flicker of hope in the midst of despair.

Chapter 7

Jessica

"And you're on your way," Mr. Jones said, gesturing toward a sleek black vehicle parked nearby. "Best of luck, Miss Jessica." His tone was laced with a condescension that made my stomach twist.

As I opened the backseat door, a wave of anxiety washed over me. I stepped inside, and my heart sank when I noticed that Camilla was already waiting for me. Her expression was serious, and without hesitation, she began to speak, her voice steady and authoritative. "From here, you'll be headed to the holding facility. You'll be in isolation until your next center is prepared. No phone, no personal belongings, nothing extra. You'll have movies and books available for your use, but don't expect any comfort beyond that. I'll return on the day your next center is set for your arrival." She paused, her lips curling into a wry smile. "For some inexplicable reason, it could take a week or two; apparently, the man pursuing you must be too busy to monitor any of the houses right now," she chuckled lightly, "or he simply enjoys putting you in isolation."

"Are you saying I'm going to be a wife?" I asked, shaking my head in disbelief. The thought felt foreign and uncomfortable. I hadn't done anything remarkable to prove I was worthy of being a wife. In truth, I hadn't achieved anything noteworthy at all.

Camilla shook her head, her auburn hair catching the dim light. "Yes, no matter how long it takes for you to win a center, this man is prepared to wait for you. He has a patience that can only be described as unnerving."

"Who is he?" I inquired, bewildered and desperate for any scrap of information.

"I thought you were clever," Camilla retorted with a hint of irritation. "I don't even know who he is. Why would you be entitled to such information? It's part of the game, Jessica."

The car rolled down the quiet street, and I shifted in my seat, my palms clammy against my jeans.

"How can I prepare for this?" I asked, staring out at the blur of houses passing by. Each one seemed to whisper secrets I wasn't meant to hear.

"You have to adapt," Camilla replied, her voice clipped. "Know your strengths and play them."

"Strengths? What strengths?" I scoffed, turning to face her. "I'm just... me."

Her gaze hardened. "Exactly. That's what you need to embrace. You've got a brilliant mind and a way with words. Use those."

I sighed, biting back frustration. "And what if that's not enough? What if he wants someone else?

Someone perfect like Allison?"

Camilla arched an eyebrow. "Allison's looks aren't going to save her when it matters most. Focus on what makes you different." She leaned closer, intensity radiating from her.

"I don't even know who he is!" My voice cracked slightly, betraying the nerves bubbling inside me.

"It doesn't matter right now," she said sharply, leaning back into her seat as the car turned onto a quieter road. "What matters is how you present yourself when you finally meet him."

"Right." I felt my heart racing again at the thought of meeting this mystery man who would decide my fate.

"Confidence," Camilla insisted, pinching her lips together like she was suppressing a laugh. "It'll take you further than you think."

"Easier said than done," I muttered under my breath.

She smirked, crossing her arms. "Oh please, I'm sure you've had your share of crushes and heartbreaks; if anyone knows how to put on a show for someone who could be judging your every move, it's you."

I hesitated, considering her words. "You really think so?"

"I know so," she replied firmly, fixing me with a determined look that sent warmth through my chest despite the situation we were in.

"What about Mia and Grace?" The question slipped out before I could stop it. My mind wandered to my best friends and our plans that seemed so far away now.

"They are not your concern right now." Camilla's voice dropped slightly as she gestured toward the driver to indicate we were almost there.

"I can't just forget about them," I insisted.

"Then don't." Camilla shot back with a spark in her eye that reminded me how fierce she could be. "But don't let thoughts of others drown out your own voice."

After what felt like a painfully long ten-minute drive, we arrived at a dimly lit apartment complex that loomed ominously in the fading light. "Home sweet home," Camilla laughed, a sound devoid of real warmth. "Go on, someone at the entrance will direct you to your room." I hesitated, the weight of uncertainty pressing heavily on my chest as I stepped out of the vehicle and into my uncertain future.

∞∞∞∞

The man at the entrance greeted me warmly, his smile almost disarming. "Miss Jessica? We've been expecting you." His voice was reassuring as he guided me towards an elevator, the polished metal doors sliding open with a soft ding. The ride up to the fifth floor felt longer than it should have, the silence between us heavy with unasked questions and unspoken fears.

"Do you know how long I'll be staying?" I inquired softly, my voice barely above a whisper, as if saying it too loudly would make it more real.

He shook his head slowly, a hint of sympathy in his eyes. "I don't have much information." With that, he opened the door to the apartment and stepped inside, closing it behind us with a definitive click. "Cameras are only outside the room. There are no cameras or audio recording devices in here. You'll be here for at least two weeks, possibly longer. This unit has been reserved for you indefinitely. Whoever is waiting for you will wait for eternity."

I took a moment to survey the compact apartment, my heart racing. It featured a small but cozy bedroom, a living area that felt slightly sterile, a nice bathroom with gleaming fixtures, and an eat-in kitchen that seemed functional enough. "How do I get food and other necessities?" I asked, hoping for some semblance of normalcy.

"They will be delivered daily," he replied gently, as if he were trying to ease the weight of the situation. "There's an intercom button at the door; you must check in every morning and evening, or we will come looking for you. Unfortunately, the door is always locked. You can use the intercom for any inquiries, food orders, and requests for movies or books."

I nodded, absorbing his words. "When will my belongings arrive?"

"Your items will be held for your next center; everything you need should be in here. If there's anything specific you require, just call down." He opened a small closet, revealing a full wardrobe that looked surprisingly well stocked. "All your personal hygiene products have been stocked in the bathroom. We will do our best to ensure this is as painless as possible."

With that, he excused himself, leaving me alone in this unfamiliar space. I felt the loneliness creep in almost instantly. I reached into the closet and grabbed a pair of sweatpants and a t-shirt, the fabric comforting against my skin as I changed quickly. I made my way to the kitchen, my stomach growling in protest.

Fortunately, there was a frozen pizza in the freezer. I tossed it into the oven, watching it sizzle as I turned on the TV. Flipping through the channels, I settled on a children's movie, its bright colors and cheerful music a stark contrast to the turmoil swirling in my mind. Just in time, I pulled the pizza out, the smell wafting through the air and momentarily distracting me from my thoughts.

After enjoying a pizza dinner and a movie marathon, I climbed into bed, the sheets cool against my skin. I pondered the man who had sent me to this place.

Why would someone desire a wife but not want to have her right away? Was he a cruel man who found pleasure in watching me suffer? Surely, a man wouldn't choose me as a wife just to torment me, would he?

The thought of isolation was daunting, gnawing at my insides, but I decided I could make the best of this situation for a few weeks. Perhaps I could find a way to cope, to survive, before finally meeting the man responsible for this ordeal. I closed my eyes, hoping that tomorrow might bring some clarity, or at the very least, a diversion from the unsettling reality I now faced.

Chapter 8

Connor

It had been 19 long days since I last beheld Jess' lovely visage, and each day felt like an eternity. Nineteen days since that despicable man had struck her, shattering her spirit and mine in the process. Nineteen days since I had personally contacted the center administrator and yelled at them for the injustice of harming a woman who was designated as my wife. Today, at long last, she would be arriving at center #3303, and my eagerness to see her once more surged within me like a tidal wave.

"Hey, the stream has been connected to your living room TV and the staff quarters TV," Jonathan announced as he stepped into my office, his voice breaking through my thoughts.

I nodded in response, the emotions swirling within me like a storm of anticipation and anxiety. "How is everyone adjusting, Jonathan?"

I had made the decision to appoint Carolynn as my house cook and Shane as the house electrician after they had been removed from the center. It felt not just appropriate, but essential, to give them a sense of purpose in this new chapter of their lives—one that had been so abruptly interrupted.

"Carolynn is fantastic; she's absolutely thrilled to be cooking and has found a true sense of purpose," Jonathan updated me, a hint of admiration evident in his tone as he spoke. "Shane, on the other hand, is quite perplexed. He doesn't fully grasp why he's here. The first task you've assigned him is to set up these TVs, but he seems uncertain about what to make of it all."

I let out a deep sigh, the weight of responsibility pressing heavily on my shoulders as I pushed myself to my feet. The thought of Jess arriving at her new center filled me with a mix of urgency and concern. "I think it's only right that I brief everyone before Jess gets here," I said, determination settling in as I prepared to face the challenge ahead. With that, I descended the staircase, each step echoing the rhythm of my quickening heartbeat. The anticipation coursed through me, a mix of excitement and apprehension as I approached the living room, where the weight of the moment loomed larger with every stride.

Upon entering, I found Shane and Carolynn engaged in a quiet conversation, their heads bent together in a moment of camaraderie that hinted at a shared understanding. The soft murmur of their exchange faded as I stepped into the room, and they both looked up at me, expressions shifting from surprise to respect, their eyes reflecting the seriousness of the situation.

"Sir," they both acknowledged me in unison as I walked in, a hint of formality lingering in their voices.

"It's Connor; there's no need to call me Sir," I replied warmly, hoping to ease any tension that might be hanging in the air. I wanted them to feel comfortable, to know that we were all in this together. "Please, everyone take a seat; I have something important to discuss." I gestured toward the chairs, trying to convey a sense of urgency without overwhelming them.

Shane appeared anxious, his body language betraying his unease as he shifted from foot to foot, his hands fidgeting at his sides. I could sense his apprehension, the weight of our collective responsibility pressing on him as much as it was on me. But just then, Jonathan nudged him playfully, a mischievous grin spreading across his face. "Just relax, man; it's merely a staff meeting," he chuckled, trying to lighten the mood. His easygoing nature often served as a balm in tense situations, and I appreciated the effort, even if it felt like the gravity of our discussion loomed over us all.

I inhaled deeply, gathering my thoughts before beginning my address. "As you know, both Carolynn and Shane, you came from the same center. I'm not sure if you've noticed, but I haven't watched any centers since that one. In fact, there are only two centers I've monitored, and the three of you are from them. Today, we will be watching another center; my future wife is about to enter it. She is the reason you are here, and we will all take turns monitoring the stream to ensure her safety. The decision for her to enter this center was also mine, and there will be another individual from this center joining our household—one of my future wife's closest childhood friends."

Carolynn was the first to respond, her eyes wide with surprise as she stammered, searching for the right words that seemed to elude her. "Wait... what?" she finally managed, shaking her head in disbelief as if trying to process my revelation. "Who?"

"It's a long tale," I began, feeling the weight of my emotions as I spoke. "But I love her. Although I've never met her, I love her deeply and will protect her with every ounce of my being." The conviction in my voice was unwavering, a shield against any doubts that might arise. "In my home, I believe in equality, trust, and respect above all else. You were all chosen for those reasons, for the values I hold dear. Jess embodies those qualities in a way that inspires me, and anyone who is important to her can hopefully find sanctuary in this home—a safe haven where they can thrive without fear."

Shane's eyes widened in disbelief, a mix of shock and confusion washing over his face. "Jessica?" he blinked, struggling to wrap his mind around the revelation. "Jessica is the one you claimed as a spouse? Jessica was claimed by you?" The weight of his words hung in the air, and I could sense the tumult of emotions swirling within him.

I confirmed with a nod, feeling a surge of pride and protectiveness surge through me. "Yes. Shane, I also owe you an explanation. While you were officially hired as my electrician, my small staff doesn't genuinely require an electrician. You were brought here to serve as Jess' security detail once she arrives." It felt crucial to clarify my intentions, to assure him that his role was not only vital but deeply valued.

Carolynn, sitting nearby, beamed with uncontainable enthusiasm, her smile infectious and lighting up the dim room. "I knew Jess was extraordinary. She's the reason I have this incredible assignment?" Her excitement radiated, and it was clear how much she cared for Jessica, mirroring my own feelings.

"But..." Shane stammered, his voice shaky as he grappled with the implications. "I could have saved her. I could have helped her go further. Why me?" The vulnerability in his tone struck a chord; he wanted to be the hero, to prove his worth.

I shook my head firmly, my expression serious. "Because you are intelligent, qualified, and you care about her. That's exactly why I chose you." It was essential that he understood his value in this mission, that he had a crucial part to play in Jessica's safety and happiness.

Jonathan simply grinned, his eyes sparkling with mischief, always ready to lighten the mood. "I knew you loved her, man. Now, do we have any snacks before we watch our girl tonight?" His playful tone cut through the tension, reminding us of the camaraderie we shared.

Carolynn sprang up, her enthusiasm palpable, as she exclaimed, "I'm sorry, I'll get them." She dashed toward the kitchen, her eagerness to contribute evident.

"No need to apologize!" I called after her, a warm smile creeping onto my face. "Jonathan, why don't you go assist that lovely girl with the snacks you just made her feel guilty about?" It felt good to share a laugh amidst the intensity of the moment.

Without a moment's hesitation, Jonathan jumped up, leaving Shane and me alone in the living room, the air thick with anticipation and an electric sense of purpose that pulsed between us.

"You alright?" I settled beside Shane on the couch, concern etched on my face as I observed his troubled expression.

He shook his head, looking up at me with tears brimming in his eyes, a mixture of disbelief and admiration swirling within. "You know, you're the kind of guy we all dreamed about as kids? We were told those dreams were pointless, that people like you didn't exist." His words struck a chord, and I felt a surge of responsibility to be the person he believed I could be.

I patted him on the back, trying to instill some hope in him. "We're just getting started, Shane. This house has been empty for two years, anticipating this moment. I will fill this home with so much love you won't know what hit you." My voice was steady, filled with the promise of the future we were about to create.

Our conversation was abruptly cut short by the sound of the

center's stream beginning, the screen flickering to life and casting a soft glow in the dim room. "Jonathan! Carolynn! Get in here!" Shane shouted, the urgency in his voice echoing the excitement that electrified the air around us.

Chapter 9

Jessica

I stepped out of the holdover facility, feeling as though I had been exiled from society for ages. I couldn't shake off the fixation on why the man who claimed me despised me so intensely. What had I done to deserve this

"Earth to Jessica," Camilla shouted from the car, her voice cutting through my fog of thoughts. "Let's go!"

I hurried over, my heart racing, and swiftly climbed into the black SUV, the leather seats cool against my skin. "Sorry," I mumbled, feeling the weight of her gaze on me.

She scrutinized me, her eyes narrowing with a mix of concern and impatience. "You look terrible, Jessica. Get it together or Mr. Moneybags might reconsider." Her words stung, but the truth in them felt undeniable. I was a mess, my emotions swirling like a storm inside me, and I knew I had to pull myself together before I faced whatever lay ahead.

I sank into the seat, the engine's low rumble vibrating through me. Camilla glanced at me from the driver's seat, her auburn hair catching the sunlight like a flame.

"You need to focus," she said, her voice sharp. "You can't afford distractions.

"I know," I replied, trying to meet her gaze "It's just… everything feels so overwhelming right now.

"Overwhelming? Try nerve-wracking." She gripped the seat tighter.

"Do you think I can actually do this?" I stared out the window at passing trees, their branches a blur of green and brown.

Camilla snorted, shaking her head slightly. "You've got the brains for it. Just channel that romantic nonsense into strategy." She glanced at me again, her expression softening for a moment. "And stop worrying about what other people did or didn't do."

"But what if I fail? What if——"

"Enough with the 'what ifs.' " she cut in, her tone firm but not unkind. "You're Jessica, and you have your own strengths."

I bit my lip, fighting back frustration. "Easy for you to say. You're not the one who has to prove herself."

"You think I didn't feel that pressure?" Camilla snapped back, eyes flashing with an intensity that made me flinch. "I did what I had to do to survive those Centers."

Her words hung heavy between us as we sped along the road. I thought about my own fears and insecurities gnawing at me.

"What happened?" I asked softly.

"Let's just say I learned quickly how to play their game." Her expression hardened again as if recalling some distant memory.

Silence enveloped us for a moment before she spoke again, softer this time. "Just remember—trust yourself."

I nodded slowly but could still feel doubt creeping in like an unwelcome guest.

"Look," she continued, "when we get there, put on your best face. Make them see you."

"Yeah," I murmured.

"Good." She settled back into her seat as we turned onto a winding road lined with tall pines, each twist bringing us closer to an unknown fate waiting just ahead.

I rolled my eyes. Any man capable of confining me in isolation for weeks must be a monster; I was certain I'd fare better elsewhere.

"Jessica, let's focus on what really matters. You are under close observation. I don't know the specifics, but a lot of influence was used to place you in this specific center." She sighed. "You can tell others about your time in a previous center, but I wouldn't advise it. They won't appreciate you or want to keep you around if you act like you're already the winner before the game starts."

I nodded. "Don't let it slip that I'm stuck being some jerk's wife for the rest of my life, understood? Be beautiful and charming, got it." I gazed out the window.

Fifteen minutes later, we arrived at a center that resembled the first one I had visited, except this one had two stories, giving it an air of grandeur that both excited and unnerved me.

"You're the first to arrive; your things have been delivered. Feel free to send a text before the others show up," Camilla informed me as I got out of the car, her tone brisk yet oddly comforting.

I smiled at her, grateful for her professionalism in this chaotic time. "Thank you, Camilla."

As I stepped into the center, I took my time to absorb the

surroundings, my heart racing with a mix of anticipation and anxiety. The downstairs featured a spacious living room, a dining area that looked welcoming, a kitchen that smelled faintly of something delicious, and what seemed to be the entrance to an office. The living room opened up to a stunning yard, complete with a pool glistening under the sun and a hot tub that bubbled invitingly. My spirits lifted momentarily as I dashed upstairs, eager to explore. To my delight, this house boasted three rooms, each equipped with four beds. I found my belongings in a cozy bedroom containing two sets of bunk beds, the sight of which made me feel a bit more at home. I quickly rummaged through my bag, heart pounding, and pulled out my phone.

Once I powered it on, my heart sank as I saw a few messages from Grace and Mia. They had figured out that I was no longer at the center. I swiftly typed out a message to let them know I was back, my fingers trembling slightly. Almost immediately, I received a reply, but it was disheartening—their numbers had been blocked or disconnected. I shook my head in disbelief, tears welling in my eyes. I hadn't been able to say goodbye, and now they were gone, lost in the maze of this new reality.

I heard the front door open, snapping me back to the present, and I realized I needed to compose myself. I took a deep breath and headed downstairs to greet the newcomer. To my relief, two friendly girls entered: one with bright blonde hair that bounced as she walked and the other a brunette with a warm smile. They introduced themselves as Risa and Maggie, and their friendly demeanor made me feel a little less alone.

A moment later, a cocky, nerdy short boy walked in, his confidence almost palpable. He introduced himself as

Topher before brushing us off and heading upstairs, leaving me slightly bewildered by his nonchalant attitude.

Before long, the center was bustling with people, laughter and chatter filling the air. Overwhelmed by the noise and excitement, I retreated to the kitchen, seeking solace in the familiarity of preparing some meatloaf, my hands busy as a distraction.

"Hello?" A familiar voice called from the front door, and I spun around so quickly that I dropped my spatula, my heart racing once more like a wild drum in my chest.

I could hardly believe my eyes. "Mia?" I managed to ask, my voice barely above a whisper, disbelief washing over me like a wave.

"Jessica?" She replied, looking just as bewildered as I felt, her eyes wide with surprise and relief, as if she had just stumbled upon a long-lost treasure.

I rushed over and pulled her in a tight hug, the warmth of her presence erasing the tension that had built over the past weeks. "Oh my god, Mia! I can't believe you're here." My words tumbled out in a rush, filled with the relief and joy of reconnecting with my best friend amidst all the chaos.

"Me? You left weeks ago. When you stopped texting, we figured you were gone somewhere. What are you doing here?" Mia's voice trembled, a mixture of confusion and concern etched on her face.

I dashed back to the kitchen, adrenaline surging as I pulled the meatloaf out of the oven before it burned. "I was chosen as a spouse. I've been in a holding facility since I got kicked out,"

I explained breathlessly, my heart aching as I recounted my experience.

I sliced a piece of meatloaf for Mia and another for myself, then carried them to the kitchen table, the warm aroma wrapping around us like a comforting embrace. We chatted for a while, catching each other up on everything we had missed, the familiar rhythm of our friendship easing the weight of our circumstances until the rest of the group came downstairs to join us for dinner, the laughter and chatter bringing a sense of normalcy back to the chaos.

Reclining at opposite ends of the bed, Mia shook her head, her brow furrowing with concern as she asked, "So, you're getting married? And you believe he's some twisted sadist who is intentionally keeping you in the centers to punish you?"

I nodded, the weight of my words heavy on my heart, pressing down like a leaden shroud. "Yes, and you can't underestimate the centers." I glanced down at my scarred knuckles, the evidence of my struggles etched into my skin like a map of my past. Each mark told a story of defiance and pain, reminders of battles fought in the shadows. "Or the Center liaisons.

Everything we do is monitored; if you're not good enough, you'll face consequences." The thought sent a shiver down my spine, recalling the relentless scrutiny that felt like a thousand eyes boring into my soul.

"Are you alright, Jessica?" Mia reached out, her hand warm and comforting as she tried to take mine, a gesture that should have brought solace but instead made my heart race with a mix of longing and dread. "How badly did they hurt you?"

I quickly pulled my hand away, a reflex born from fear and the instinct to protect myself—a self-preservation mechanism that had become second nature. "I'm fine. I'll be fine. I just need you to do whatever it takes to stay safe here." My voice was steadier than my insides felt, the words tumbling out with a fragile façade of confidence, masking the turmoil that churned beneath the surface.

She smiled, though it didn't quite reach her eyes. "I'm tougher than you think. I'm hoping to prove myself useful as a cleaner or an assistant." Her determination was admirable, yet it made me question my own resolve.

When did she figure out her objective with the centers? Why hadn't I found a way forward? Maybe if I had tried harder to be useful, I wouldn't have ended up claimed by this man who seemed determined to torment me before our wedding. The thought of him sent a wave of unease crashing over me.

"Earth to Jessica. You seem so different; what's going on in that head of yours?" Mia poked me playfully in the side, trying to draw me back into the moment.

"Nothing, I just…" I hesitated, searching for the right words, "I wish I had shown that I could be something." The admission felt like a weight lifted, yet it also deepened the chasm of my despair.

Mia blurted, "You're going to be a wife; you're going to be free. Why are you so scared?" Her voice carried a hint of anger, an emotion I understood all too well. "Did that man send someone to take you for a trial run? I didn't think the Liaisons allowed that anymore. They didn't do that in the holding facility, did they? I'll kill them; they can't do that." The fierceness of her protectiveness struck a chord within me.

I reached out instinctively, my palm pressing against her mouth, desperate to silence her. "Shhh, if they hear you, no one will want you as their servant." My whisper was urgent, laden with the weight of our precarious situation, the consequences of which loomed over us like a dark cloud.

"Sorry," Mia muttered, her eyes darting around the room as if the very walls might betray us with their silent secrets. Her anxiety radiated from her, thick and tangible. "But…"

I shook my head, cutting her off before her words could spiral further. "No, Mia, they didn't. Though I guess they probably will before I'm married, huh?" The resignation in my voice hung heavy in the air, a bitter aftertaste of defeat that I couldn't shake off.

Mia shrugged, her expression a tumultuous blend of frustration and empathy, as if she was grappling with her own helplessness in this tangled web we found ourselves in. Just as I was about to speak again, the moment was abruptly shattered by the entrance of Risa and Maggie, their laughter and lively chatter spilling into the room like sunlight piercing through the gloom.

"Are we interrupting?" Maggie asked, her perceptive nature quickly picking up on the tension that had settled in the room, thick and stifling like a heavy fog.

I stood up, forcing a smile that felt foreign on my lips, a fragile façade to mask the turmoil roiling inside

me. "No, just getting to know each other," I said, my voice brightening in an attempt to dispel the shadows. "But I should get ready for bed. Tomorrow will be a long day."

The thought of the next day loomed over me, heavy and unyielding. If I learned anything from my first experience with the centers, it was that this entire ordeal was going to be hell—an agonizing test of endurance and will that I wasn't sure I could survive.

∞∞∞∞

I couldn't tell if it was a nightmare, déjà vu, or if I was genuinely waking up to experience this all over again, my heart racing with a mix of dread and confusion.

"You have 30 minutes to locate all the puzzle pieces. The winner stays another day; the others may be eliminated," the unmistakable robotic voice blared through the loudspeaker, its cold, mechanical tone echoing in the sterile room. "You have 30 minutes to locate all the puzzle pieces. The winner stays another day; the others may be eliminated."

I tumbled out of bed, the sheets tangling around my legs, and realized I must have missed part of the announcement because Mia, Risa, and Maggie had already overturned their beds with frantic urgency and disappeared into the chaos.

I reached beneath my mattress, my fingers brushing against the cool, hard surface, and discovered a puzzle piece with a note attached to the back—a rarity in this place. This one was different; there had never been a note before. I stuffed it into my pocket, feeling its weight, and dashed into the bathroom, my heart pounding in my chest. I searched frantically for another piece, my breath quickening as I found one hidden under the toilet seat, a perfect little secret buried in this bleak environment. Just before I exited the stall, I felt the note brush against my knuckles, a soft reminder of the mystery unfolding around me.

Curiosity overwhelmed me, and I bent down to retrieve the note, my hands trembling slightly as I unfolded it.

"It will all be worth it, Jess. CD." I stared at the mysterious message several times, my mind racing with questions. Who could have written this? Who was CD? How did this note find its way under my bed? The initials felt familiar yet elusive, teasing the edges of my memory.

Before I could resume my search for the remaining pieces, the announcement blared again, cutting through my thoughts; all the pieces had been collected, and we needed to place them in our lockers for counting. I tucked the note into my bra, convinced that if the Center discovered it, I would be in deep trouble, my heart sinking at the thought of consequences.

Once I was back in bed, I tried to piece things together in my mind, the chaos of the moment swirling around me. "Carolynn? Could it be from Carolynn? Maybe she was working at the Center and managed to slip it to me?" The possibilities danced in my head, but the weight of uncertainty pressed down on me.

Before I realized what was happening, exhaustion took over, and I had drifted off again, the promise of answers slipping further away into the abyss of sleep.

Chapter 10

Connor

I never imagined that sending her to the holding facility for such an extended period would affect her so profoundly. The sight of her—frightened, worn out, and utterly distressed—was a gut punch I hadn't prepared for. All I could do was cling to the hope that the note I had paid an outrageous sum to slip under Jessica's bed would somehow make a difference, that it would bridge the chasm of fear and doubt that had formed between us.

As if he could sense my turmoil, Jonathan chimed in, his voice steady but tinged with concern. "We're not going to hold her again if she doesn't win this center, right? I mean, she definitely didn't win that competition." His words echoed in my mind, a reminder of the precarious situation we were in.

I shook my head, trying to dispel the weight of my worries. "No, we can't subject her to that long of isolation again." The thought of her enduring that loneliness again made my stomach churn.

Carolynn moved toward the kitchen, her gentle hand patting my shoulder in a gesture of reassurance. "You're doing the right thing, sir. She's going to be grateful for it." Her belief in my choices was comforting, but it felt like a fragile lifeline amidst the chaos.

"She sees me as a monster," I murmured, the confession slipping out before I could stop it. My heart felt like it was collapsing under the weight of everything that had transpired in the last twelve hours. "And putting her in the center with Mia, maybe that wasn't the best choice." The thought of how they must have reacted to each other gnawed at me.

The pesky little boy, Topher, had eavesdropped on Jess and Mia's chat the previous night, his tiny ears absorbing every word. He knew they were friends and that she was already slated for marriage. He had already shared the news with some of the other boys in his room—loud, boisterous boys who didn't even know her but had quickly formed an opinion that she didn't belong there, as if they had the right to judge her fate.

"No," Shane interrupted as he walked into the living room, his voice firm and resolute. "She needed to see a friend." His tone faded as he sank onto the couch, the weight of his own thoughts evident on his face.

I nodded, attempting to convince myself that we had made the right decision. "I'm going to go rest; wake me when she's up again." With that, I turned away, hoping that when I opened my eyes again, everything would be brighter, that my choices would lead to healing rather than further heartache.

Jessica

I stirred awake to the sensation of Mia prodding me gently. "Hey, sleepyhead. Time to get up. I made eggs," she said, her voice cheerful and bright, cutting through the haze of my dreams.

With a groggy nod, I swung my legs over the side of the bed and rubbed the sleep from my eyes. "Thanks, Mia," I mumbled, feeling a rush of gratitude for her ever-present kindness. I padded over to my locker, the cool metal a stark contrast to the warmth of my blankets, and retrieved a light purple dress that hung neatly on the hook. I paired it with some flip flops that had seen better days but still felt comfortable on my feet.

As I approached the makeup table, I took a moment to appreciate the array of colors and products laid out before me. I picked up a few essentials—a soft foundation, a touch of blush, and a swipe of mascara—applying just a hint of light makeup. I wasn't one to go all out; bold colors and heavy eyeliner felt foreign to me. But a little touch could make a noticeable difference in how I felt, infusing me with a sense of confidence as I prepared for the day ahead. Satisfied with my reflection, I gave my hair a quick toss and headed downstairs, anticipation fluttering in my stomach like a dozen butterflies, eager for whatever moments awaited me.

Upon entering the kitchen, I scanned the room, noting the mix of unfamiliar faces surrounding the table. I realized I didn't even know most of these individuals' names. There were six guys present, including the irritating Topher, whose smirk from yesterday still lingered in my mind.

"Hey," I greeted the girls scattered around, trying to muster some semblance of cheerfulness.

Risa was the first to respond, her voice warm and inviting. "Good morning."

"Ohhh, look who decided to grace us with her presence," Topher shouted, his tone dripping with sarcasm as I took a seat, trying to ignore the prickling heat of embarrassment creeping up my neck.

Before I could formulate a witty comeback to slice through his mockery, an announcement rang out over the chatter, declaring that Topher had won this morning's challenge and was required to report to the office. The room fell silent for a moment, and I felt a flicker of satisfaction at his sudden distraction.

When he returned, he wore a smug expression, his eyes zeroed in on me like a hawk spotting its prey. I could feel my heart rate quicken under his intense gaze, and I steeled myself for whatever taunt was about to come.

"Spit it out, Topher," I finally retorted, crossing my arms defiantly over my chest, trying to exude confidence despite the fluttering anxiety in my stomach. "Do you have an issue with me?"

"Oh, your highness, of course I do," he hissed, leaning in close enough that I could see the gleam of mischief in his eyes, as if he relished the thought of pushing my buttons. His smirk was infuriating, and I could feel my patience wearing thin.

Before I could react, my arm shot up, seemingly driven by instinct, as I aimed to shove him back with a show of defiance. But in an instant, Topher grabbed my wrist with an iron grip, yanking me down to the ground, his knee pressing into my back. "Ow," I cried out in pain, the suddenness of it all catching me completely off guard, and I felt a surge of frustration mixed with vulnerability wash over me.

"What the hell?" Mia jumped up, her face a mask of concern as she hurried over, closely followed by Rissa, who looked equally alarmed.

Topher released me, standing up with an air of satisfaction. "Someone needs to teach this bitch her place," he muttered with a snarl, his words hanging thick in the air between us.

Just as the tension reached its peak, an announcement broke through: "The two at risk of being eliminated are

Jessica and Mia. Everyone, please gather around the dining table to meet your Center Liaison."

We all quickly took our seats, murmurs of confusion and fear rippling through the group.

The front door creaked open, and a familiar figure stepped in—Mr. Jones. "Well, hello, nice to meet you all. I am your Center Liaison here to help guide you," he said, his voice smooth yet laced with authority.

"Yes, sir," we all replied in unison, the weight of his presence settling heavily in the room.

He called out six names, and I felt a wave of relief wash over me, thankful that Mia and I were excluded from his list. Those six were informed that as a consequence for not being entertaining enough, their beds would be reduced to mere wooden frames—an unsettling fate that sent shivers down my spine. Soon, Mr. Jones finished expressing his frustration and excused himself with a dismissive wave.

As the room filled with the buzz of anxious chatter, I felt the need to escape the suffocating atmosphere. I pulled Mia upstairs, seeking refuge from the prying ears below. "Mia, I'm the one these people are targeting," I said, my voice barely above a whisper but tinged with urgency. "You need to keep proving yourself." The words spilled out, laced with the desperation of my situation.

She shook her head, her expression resolute and defiant. "Maybe there's another way," she countered, her eyes ablaze with a fierce determination that both inspired and worried me.

I shrugged, trying to mask the weight of reality pressing down on my shoulders. "My fate is sealed," I replied, the resignation in my tone matching the heaviness in my heart. "You need to fight for yours, Mia. Fight for the life you desire." I urged her, hoping she could grasp the gravity of what we were facing.

The stakes were high, and I needed her to see that this wasn't just about me; it was about all of us.

Chapter 11

Jessica

Before I realized it, I was wrapped in Mia's warm embrace as we said our tearful goodbyes. The world around us faded into a blur, and I clung to her, hoping to freeze this moment in time, but then Mr. Jones was there, forcefully pushing me out the door. Once outside, the weight of reality crashed down on me, and I sank to the cold, hard ground, tears streaming down my cheeks.

"This can't be the last time I see her," I cried, my voice trembling with despair.

Mr. Jones huffed dismissively, "Foolish girl... You're someone else's issue now," and with that, he stormed off, leaving me feeling more alone than ever.

After a moment of wallowing in my sorrow, I glanced up to see him in the walkway, engaged in a heated discussion with Camilla. Their bodies were tense, and it was evident they were in the midst of a fierce argument, words exchanged like daggers thrown in the air.

Camilla's eyes flicked toward me, and she hurriedly motioned for Mr. Jones to leave. "Come on, Jessica. Don't let him get to you; that was painful to witness today." She extended her hand to help me up, her expression a mixture of concern and determination.

"Thank you," I said, accepting her assistance gratefully, feeling her strength bolster my own. "What now?"

She grinned, a spark of mischief lighting up her face. "Back to the holding facility." She began guiding me toward the waiting SUV, her steps confident and purposeful.

"For how long?" I grimaced at the prospect of spending weeks there again, the sterile walls and the oppressive atmosphere closing in on me.

Camilla chuckled lightly, "Oh, you silly dear, it'll only be a few days. You've caught the center hunter's attention, and they're moving you to an accelerated center. Someone's eager to get their hands on you." Her tone was teasing, but I could hear an undercurrent of seriousness beneath it.

With a resigned sigh, I flopped into the SUV, the leather seat cool against my skin. This man must truly despise me to put me through this, and the thought churned in my stomach, mixing with the fear of the unknown that lay ahead.

∞∞∞∞∞

Before long, we arrived back at the holding facility, and Camilla granted me the liberty to step out on my own. A familiar face awaited me at the entrance—the same man I had encountered during my initial visit to the facility.

"Jessica, it saddens me to see you back. Especially so soon; what happened?" he inquired, opening the door and ushering me inside, directing me toward the elevator.

I shook my head, my heart heavy with frustration. "Someone really had it out for me."

As we stepped into the elevator, I noticed him fidgeting, his fingers twitching nervously as he waited for the doors to close. Once they finally did, he turned to me, his expression a mix of concern and empathy. "My name is Brad. I came from the centers too. I'm just... I'm sorry." He paused as if searching for the right words. "They suck; this all sucks."

A warmth spread through me, and I couldn't help but smile. Before I knew it, laughter bubbled up, harder and more genuine than I had experienced in quite some time, prompting Brad to chuckle along with me. "It's nice to officially meet you, Brad. Yes, this really does suck."

We shared a few more laughs, the tension easing just a bit, until he finally pressed the button for my floor. "Just a heads up, Jessica, your kitchen has been restocked and some additional items have been provided. It's clear someone very special is keeping an eye on you."

"I don't understand," I exclaimed, the words tumbling out in a rush. "Is this typical?"

Just then, the elevator came to a sudden halt, and the doors slid open with a quiet ding. A well-dressed twenty-year-old blonde man stood waiting, his displeased expression and bloodied knuckles sending a chill down my spine.

"Oh good, staff," he greeted Brad with a dismissive wave. "That one is not acceptable. It's a shame she could have won a center. See that she's cleaned up before being returned to a center, and now she's been rejected. She won't be a winner."

"Yes, Mr. Kline," Brad responded promptly, his voice steady yet betraying an underlying tension that I could sense radiating from him.

As I felt the man's gaze fixate on me, an unsettling chill crept up my spine, like icy fingers skimming over my skin. I kept my eyes down, focusing intently on Brad's shoes, willing myself to become invisible in that moment, to disappear from the scrutiny. "Is this one available for a test drive?" he asked, his hand reaching out with an unsettling confidence to touch my hair above my ear. The predatory glint in his eyes sent a wave of nausea through me.

Before I could even gather my thoughts to react, Brad swiftly seized the man's hand, yanking it away with a forcefulness that surprised me. "She is not to be touched, sir. She is not available," he asserted, his voice low but firm, a shield standing between me and that man's unsettling intentions.

With that, Brad protectively placed his hand on my shoulder, a reassuring weight that urged me to keep moving, guiding me out of the elevator and down a dimly lit hallway, away from the oppressive atmosphere and toward safety.

As we walked away, I heard the man shout behind us, his voice dripping with disdain, "Pity, I deserved something tonight after coming all the way out here." The words hung in the air like a threatening cloud, and I quickened my pace, my heart pounding in my chest.

Once we rounded a corner, Brad paused, signaling for me to be quiet until he listened for the sound of the elevator doors closing and descending. "Sorry. Can never be too cautious," he whispered, his eyes darting around the corner, scanning for any sign of danger. "Coast is clear. Come on."

I followed him in silence, my heart racing, acutely aware of the danger that loomed just behind us, the remnants of that man's gaze still lingering in my mind. Once we were safely inside my suite, I broke the heavy silence that enveloped us. "Who was he? What was happening?"

"You weren't meant to see that. I'm really sorry," Brad said, shaking his head as he reached for the doorknob, his expression grave and filled with concern.

I stepped forward, blocking his path, determination surging within me. "Tell me what's going on. I deserve to know," I insisted, my voice steady despite the turmoil churning inside me.

Brad sighed, the weight of unspoken worries etched on his face. "I'm here as a protector of the girls. This is primarily a holding facility, but the suites are also used for trial competitions."

"Trial competitions? I thought those weren't allowed anymore," I questioned, my mind racing as I tried to grasp the implications.

Now it was his turn to look down, his gaze heavy with regret. "They tell us that in school to keep us in line. They aren't forced anymore, but when someone reaches the final four spots, potential spouses can request a sexual trial competition. The individual can refuse to participate, which is likely what happened, and typically they are then rejected."

"So that man? He wanted to try a girl, and she said no?" The realization hit me like a cold wave.

Brad nodded solemnly. "And he probably hit her, which lowers the chances that her other potential husbands will accept her. No one wants a wife who is battered and unwilling to prove she can perform."

I shook my head in disbelief. "Wow, this place really does suck."

Brad nodded, his expression softening as he moved toward

the door. "Most of the time, but you're our glimmer of hope." He smiled gently, a flicker of warmth in the bleakness. "Check the bedroom, Jessica. Goodnight."

After the door closed behind him, I walked to the bedroom, my heart still racing. I peeked inside and was taken aback to discover dozens of blue hydrangea bouquets filling the room, their vibrant petals a stark contrast to the sterile environment. In the center, a note lay waiting, and I lifted it up, reading it slowly, my mind struggling to process the words: "I cannot wait until you are home with me."

I dropped the note in shock, my heart pounding erratically in my chest. Who was this man? How did he know my favorite flowers? And what was he planning to do with me? My mind raced with fear of the trials ahead and the dread of this man who seemed to know everything about me, his intentions shrouded in a mystery that left me both terrified and intrigued.

Chapter 12

Jessica

I spent the following three days treating myself to all my favorite dishes, snacks, and films, reveling in the comfort of familiar indulgences that brought a sense of normalcy amid the chaos. I binge-watched shows that made me laugh and cry, each episode a buoy in a sea of uncertainty, while I baked warm, gooey chocolate chip cookies that filled the apartment with their sweet, inviting aroma, wrapping me in a nostalgic embrace. The simple act of licking the bowl of brownie batter—my guilty pleasure— brought me a fleeting sense of joy, a small rebellion against the world outside, as if I could hold onto a piece of childhood innocence for just a little longer. Long, luxurious baths became my sanctuary, where I could escape from reality; the warm water enveloped me like a cocoon, soothing my frayed nerves and allowing me to drift away from the looming dread. I even managed to squeeze in a bit of exercise, although I couldn't say I was particularly committed; it felt more like a distraction than a true effort, a way to keep my mind off the impending unknown.

To my surprise, several of my cherished books had arrived in my bedroom, their spines already worn from anticipation, as if they had been waiting for me to dive into their pages. At one point, I found myself so engrossed in a werewolf romance novel that I lost track of time, spending over an hour in the tub, the water growing cool around me. The world outside faded away as I became lost in the story, living vicariously through the characters who faced their own challenges and found love against all odds. That night, I dreamt about discovering my "true mate" and escaping together to conquer the world, a fantasy so vivid it left me both exhilarated and unsettled. The notion upset me so much that I tossed the book aside, unable to face the story's hopeful ending, feeling as though it mocked my own reality, which felt increasingly bleak and uncertain.

But now, just four days after bidding farewell to Mia, my little vacation had come to an abrupt end as I stood at the entrance of a center that resembled the first one I had attended. The atmosphere was thick with apprehension, and I felt a flutter of anxiety in my chest, a gnawing feeling that something was off, as if the air itself was charged with unspoken fears.

Tentatively, I opened the door, my heart racing as I braced myself for what lay beyond. What greeted me was a complete kitchen, its bright lights harsh and glaring against the dimming twilight that seeped through the window. The intensity of the illumination felt almost mocking, highlighting the starkness of my new reality and the unsettling unfamiliarity that lay ahead. I took a cautious step inside, the sterile smell of disinfectant mingling with the faint aroma of something cooking, a reminder that life continued to move forward, even when I felt frozen in place.

"Hi," I announced quickly as I stepped inside, my voice a fragile echo in the unfamiliar space, betraying my nerves. My blonde hair was straightened flawlessly, framing my face with a polished sheen, and I wore a touch of subtle mascara, hoping to project a sense of confidence I didn't quite feel. I had picked a vibrant yellow and white flower from the garden when leaving the holding facility, and it now rested tucked behind my ear, a small token of beauty amidst the uncertainty that loomed around me.

The group was lively and animated, their voices blending into a symphony of chatter as they welcomed me amidst their discussions, their energy both inviting and overwhelming. A sweet brunette with bouncy curls was the first to approach me, her smile warm and inviting, a beacon of friendliness in a sea of strangers. "Hey, I'm Desiree. Come on over and join us for dinner. I love your flower!" Her enthusiasm was contagious, and I felt a flicker of warmth in my chest, a small flame of hope igniting amidst my fear.

She cleared her throat as we joined the crowd, and I felt the weight of their eyes on me, both curious and friendly, as if they were sizing me up and welcoming me all at once. "Hey, everyone. I think we need to introduce ourselves," she suggested, her enthusiasm infectious, lighting up the room even more and momentarily distracting me from my worries.

There were eight of us girls and four guys gathered around the table, and amidst the lively chatter and laughter, a few individuals distinctly caught my attention. An average-looking guy named Harry stood out with his overly friendly demeanor; he was brimming with an almost endearing cockiness about his intelligence that I found difficult to relate to. His enthusiasm seemed genuine, yet it only highlighted my own insecurities. Across the room, a bubbly blonde with curly hair, Meg, radiated an infectious energy that seemed to light up the entire space. Her laughter was bright and free, an exhilarating sound that felt like a stark contrast to the knot of apprehension twisting inside me. As I sat there, I had to consciously remind myself not to choke on my spaghetti while Meg flirted shamelessly with a very fit guy named Jake. His chiseled features made him stand out even more, and he exuded a level of confidence that seemed so effortless, serving as an unintentional reminder of the self-assurance I longed for but felt so far from ever attaining.

Before long, we were all heading to bed, the energy of the day finally catching up with me as I felt the exhaustion seep into my bones, wrapping around me like a heavy blanket. I knew tomorrow would be a long day, filled with new faces and experiences that both excited and terrified me. I hoped it would be uneventful, a simple reprieve from the chaos that had become my life, a fleeting moment of normalcy in a world turned upside down by the looming uncertainty of the Centers.

Before settling in, I tried to text Mia and Grace, my heart aching for a connection to the outside world, for a lifeline to my old life that felt increasingly distant. I needed their voices, their laughter, to remind me of who I was before all this. But both messages bounced back as undeliverable again, a stark reminder of the barriers that now separated us, leaving me feeling even more isolated in my small, dark room. It was worth a shot, but the silence felt heavy in my chest, an oppressive weight that only intensified my feelings of longing for the friendships that had once anchored me. I lay there, staring at the ceiling, wondering when I might feel whole again, when I could once more share my thoughts and fears with the girls who understood me like no one else.

Mia

It had been five long, agonizing days since Jessica left, and now I found myself stepping out of the center, the oppressive weight of it behind me, with Mr. Jones at my side.

"You, my dear Mia, are off to your post. You will be a housekeeper for a wonderful man who is building his household." He motioned toward a sleek, black BMW sedan parked nearby, its polished surface glinting in the sunlight. "Go on, his assistant is waiting for you."

I nodded slowly, a swirl of emotions churning within me. This really was it—the moment I had both dreaded and yearned for. "Thank you, sir," I managed to say, the words feeling hollow as they left my lips, but my feet did not move.

The transition was jarring and had me frozen in place. Just hours ago, Mr. Jones had wielded power like a blunt instrument, punishing people with shocking bracelets, whips and cold detachment. Now, he stood before me in that same crisp suit, a picture of professionalism as he gestured toward the car.

"Everything will be just fine," he said, his voice smooth and calculated. "Your new employer is quite eager to have you." His smile was disarming, almost friendly, but it sent a shiver down my spine.

I took a cautious step back. The man who had delighted in our suffering now acted as if he were my advocate. What twisted game was he playing? My heart raced as I forced myself to maintain eye contact. What did he mean by Eager?

"You seem uncertain." He tilted his head slightly, studying me with an unnerving intensity.

"No," I replied too quickly. I could hear the tremor in my voice. "Just... taking it all in."

His expression didn't waver. "You should consider this a new opportunity," he continued, waving his hand toward the waiting vehicle like a magician unveiling his latest trick. "A chance to shine in a role designed for someone with your... skills."

Skills? All I had were memories of fear and betrayal from the center. How could I possibly excel when every moment felt laced with danger?

"Right," I muttered under my breath. He wouldn't let me wallow in uncertainty for long; his patience ran thin when it came to anyone questioning authority.

"Go on," Mr. Jones urged with a practiced smile that didn't reach his eyes.

I hesitated but couldn't afford to linger on my doubts any longer. The thought of being alone forever, without Jessica or Grace, gnawed at me like a persistent ache. With one last glance at him—a man who could switch from sadist to mentor in an instant— I took my first step towards the rest of my life.

As I walked toward the car, a tall man emerged from around the sleek vehicle, his demeanor instantly reassuring as he opened the passenger door for me. "Hello, Ms. Mia. Nice to meet you," he said, his voice warm and inviting, contrasting sharply with the cold air that seemed to cling to me from the Center.

I climbed in, my hands trembling uncontrollably, a mix of fear and anticipation coursing through my veins like ice water. "Thank you," I mumbled, barely managing to keep my voice steady as hot tears began to stream down my cheeks. The flood of emotion was overwhelming, a release I had not anticipated, and I felt exposed and vulnerable in that moment.

He quickly settled into the driver's seat, his movements confident as he shifted the car into gear and pulled away from the Center's grim confines. The dreary building receded into the background, and I was acutely aware of the freedom that layahead. "Hey, I'm Jonathan," he said, glancing at me with a small, encouraging smile as we drove about a quarter-mile down the road. "Do you want to hit a drive-through?" His casual tone felt like an invitation to breathe, to let go of the weight I had been carrying, if only for a moment.

"Is that allowed?" I looked up at him, my heart pounding at the tantalizing thought of freedom, even if it was just for a fleeting moment. The prospect of breaking away from all those sterile walls sent a thrill coursing through me.

He laughed, the sound light and infectious, breaking the tension that had settled in the car. "Don't ask me why we got blessed with the best assignments ever. Yes, we can stop wherever you'd like." His enthusiasm was contagious, and I felt a spark of hope flicker within me.

"A burger would be nice," I answered, my stomach growling at the thought of actual food. It had been too long since I had indulged in something so simple and satisfying. "Am I allowed to ask, who is he?" The question slipped out, curiosity getting the better of me.

Jonathan took a deep breath, as if preparing to share something significant. "One burger. And of course, you can ask; you're part of the household now!" His words hung in the air, a promise of belonging that I hadn't dared to hope for.

"So..." I trailed off, uncertainty lingering like a shadow between us, the implications of his words settling in my mind.

He pulled into a burger restaurant, the tantalizing smell wafting through the air, making my mouth water as I inhaled deeply. As he placed our order, he turned to me with a playful smirk, his eyes sparkling with mischief. "You are now officially property of the house of Connor Dandin."

My mouth must have hit the floor immediately because Jonathan erupted into laughter, his joy infectious, momentarily distracting me from the gravity of my situation. I couldn't help but join in, a giggle escaping my lips, feeling the weight of my past lifting just a little in that moment of shared laughter.

Chapter 13

Jessica

The following day unfolded in a surprisingly ordinary manner, especially when I reflected on my initial experiences at the last two centers. It began with a trivia contest that had everyone buzzing with excitement. Harry, with his usual overzealous charm, emerged victorious, practically beaming with pride. His smug grin as he claimed his title was almost infuriating, and I couldn't help but roll my eyes. The leaderboard was different than past centers, leaving five individuals languishing at the bottom, including the flirty Meg. She pouted dramatically, her expression a mix of disbelief and theatrical despair as she tried to drown her low score in exaggerated sighs.

Lunch was spread on the kitchen island, the center bustling with noise. I picked at my plate, the bland pasta offering little in terms of excitement. Whoever had made this lunch hopefully wasn't trying to become a chef for their assignment. Harry, still riding high from his trivia victory, waved me over.

"Jess! You gotta try this. It's—"

I glanced at him and grimaced. "No thanks, I think I'll pass on the culinary adventure."

He laughed, tossing a piece of lettuce my way. It landed right on my shoulder.

Desiree slid into the seat across from me, her brow furrowed as she surveyed the scene. "Are you okay? You look like you just saw a ghost."

"Just Harry being Harry," I replied, brushing off the lettuce. "What about you?"

"I can't believe they let him win." She glanced toward Harry, who was now engaging Meg in some ridiculous debate about the best pizza toppings.

I chuckled softly and picked up my fork. "It's like he thinks he's on a game show or something."

The chatter around us faded into a dull roar as we ate in relative silence. After lunch, I headed back to my room for a shower. The hot water cascaded down my back, steam filling the small space. I let out a breath, trying to wash away the tension of the day. A few moments of solitude were all I craved amidst the chaos.

Once dried off and dressed in comfortable clothes, I returned to find Desiree setting up a chessboard on one of the tables in our common area.

"Ready to get schooled?" she teased, her eyes sparkling with competitive spirit.

I smirked and took a seat across from her. "In your dreams." The pieces clicked against each other as we moved them into position. The game began slowly; each of us sizing up our opponent with careful strategies.

Desiree made her first move with confidence. "You know this whole center thing isn't so bad if you find ways to keep your mind busy."

"Yeah? What do you suggest? More trivia?" I grinned as I slid my pawn forward.

She laughed lightly but then turned serious for a moment. "We could always try to escape through strategy games."

I leaned back in my chair and studied her face, intrigued by her thoughts despite their gravity amid our lighthearted game.

"Okay," I said slowly after weighing her words, "but first we have to finish this match."

Our conversation danced around various topics as we played—friendships formed under pressure and dreams of what lay beyond these walls—and before long, each piece on the board became a symbol of something bigger than just winning or losing.

Then came the subsequent competition for the three contestants, a whirlwind of tension and excitement, which was won by Meg's boy-toy. In a display of chivalry that seemed almost scripted, he utilized

his "save a friend" prize to rescue her from the depths of the rankings, pulling her up just as she seemed ready to sink into despair. It was the kind of moment that made me question the sincerity of their relationship, a spectacle that felt more like a carefully orchestrated performance than an authentic connection.

The only truly noteworthy moment of the day arrived when Mrs. Smith, our center liaison, strode into the room like she owned the place, her presence filling the space with a palpable tension. She had that fierce look about her—sharp jawline, narrowed eyes, and a posture that suggested she could have been on the wrestling team if she'd bothered to join one.

Her tailored suit clung to her form in a way that felt more intimidating than professional. With a flick of her wrist, she smoothed back her tightly pulled hair, and I wondered if she practiced her scowls in front of a mirror. She revealed that the powers that be were anxious to get us through this center quickly and four individuals would be departing for their assignments that very night. "Listen up," she barked, cutting through the murmurs of conversation. "I don't have all day."

The room fell silent. I glanced around; everyone's eyes were glued to her, wide with apprehension. I shifted in my seat, suddenly conscious of how unprepared I felt.

"Tonight," Mrs. Smith continued, "four of you will be departing for your assignments. This isn't a popularity contest or a feel-good movie." She paused, scanning our faces as if we were all guilty until proven innocent.

Her voice dripped with disdain when she addressed Harry. "And you, smart guy? Don't let your big head get you eliminated next time." He squirmed under her glare.

"Life isn't about warm fuzzies," she snapped at Meg when she dared to raise a hand with a question about the selection process. "You're here to compete, not hold hands and sing campfire songs."

My stomach knotted at the thought of being among those chosen to leave tonight. I scanned the room for familiar faces, searching for reassurance in Desiree's gaze or even in Meg's playful demeanor, but they mirrored my own uncertainty.

She called up four people—Sara, George, Lisa, and Della—each time I felt a fresh wave of dread wash over me. I had barely noticed their presence before, but as she outlined how stupid, mundane, ugly, or boring each one was, a tight knot formed in my stomach. Her words were sharp and cutting, highlighting their supposed flaws with a cruel satisfaction, and it made my heart race. It was clear that this was the reason for their departure, but it felt more like a twisted spectacle than a mere selection process. I couldn't help but wonder who would be next and whether I'd be among them.

"And let's make one thing clear," Mrs. Smith continued, punctuating each word as if driving home an essential point. "If you want to survive this center and whatever comes next, you need to show resilience." Her steely gaze landed on me briefly before moving on, but it felt like an electric shock—a reminder of my precarious position here.

With that final statement hanging heavily in the air, Mrs. Smith turned sharply on her heel and strode out of the room without another word, leaving us to grapple with what lay ahead as whispers erupted among us once more.

The four who had occupied the lowest ranks among us, stood quietly as we all bid farewell to them as swiftly as we had greeted one another. The air hung thick with a mix of relief and unspoken fears, a palpable reminder of the precariousness of our situation. Their departure was an unsettling truth that lingered in the back of my mind, a constant reminder that our fates could shift in an instant, leaving us to grapple with the unknown.

Once they were gone, we quietly gathered for dinner, the atmosphere thick with a blend of inconsequential chatter and nervous laughter, each of us trying to mask the unease gnawing at our insides. The clinking of forks and the murmur of voices felt almost surreal, as if we were playing a part in a mockery of normalcy. As the evening wore on, the weight of our circumstances loomed over us until it was finally time to retreat for the night. Predictably, Meg, ever the drama queen, proclaimed the day to be "too much," her voice rising above the subdued conversations.

She insisted that she needed to snuggle with Jake to get any sleep, her playful tone attempting to lighten the mood. I couldn't help but roll my eyes at the spectacle she made of herself, but deep down, I envied her ability to distract herself from the chaos surrounding us. Fortunately, when I finally crawled into bed, I fell asleep the moment my head hit the pillow, blissfully escaping the harsh reality of our situation, if only for a little while.

However, at some point during the night, I was jolted awake by a sound coming from the floor. Blinking a few times to clear my vision, I realized it was Desiree, crouched near her bed.

"Shhh, meet me in the bathroom in 10 minutes," she whispered urgently before crawling back into bed, her voice barely above a breath.

A short while later, she got up and stealthily made her way to the shared bathroom. My heart raced as I followed not long after, discovering her hidden away in a stall. I chose the one beside hers, keeping a vigilant eye on the camera focused on the door, acutely aware of the risks we were taking.

"So what's so urgent that you had to drag me here in the middle of the night?" I whispered, my voice barely above a whisper, laced with a mix of curiosity and concern.

She spoke softly, her tone serious. "I can't afford to take any risks. I have a message; my Center Hunter here took a chance to tell me, so it must be significant."

I was taken aback by the gravity of her words, a chill creeping down my spine as the implications settled in. If the liaisons caught wind of this—if they learned I was involved—we would both be in serious trouble, and I could only imagine the consequences. "What? Why? They're going to punish us if they find out," I hissed, glancing nervously around the dimly lit stall, anxiety tightening its grip on my chest and sending my heart racing.

"I can't make sense of any of these happenings or rules in this awful place," she shot back, her irritation evident in her tone and the way her fingers clenched into fists at her sides. "But I hear you know Grace?

She was in my last center. Can you believe it? She's been sold off in marriage." The words hung in the air, heavy with the weight of her frustration and the grim reality of our situation. My heart sank at the mention of Grace, my mind racing with worry for her well-being and what this meant for all of us.

The revelation struck me like a heavy blow, stealing my breath away and leaving me momentarily speechless. "Wait, you know Grace? Is she alright?" was all I could manage to say, a knot of dread tightening in my stomach as the reality of our situation sank in. The thought of Grace—my dear friend, so full of potential—being in jeopardy filled me with an overwhelming sense of unease, especially now that I realized Desiree was also marked for this second chance center.

"She's strong; she'll be fine," Desiree sighed, her voice tinged with uncertainty that did little to quell my fears. I could sense the worry behind her words, the way they hung heavy in the air between us. "I didn't see her after the trials. I'm sure she did better than I did." Her attempt at reassurance felt fragile, almost like a thread barely holding us together in the face of the unknown. The weight of our circumstances pressed down on me, and I found myself clinging to the hope that Grace's strength would see her through this nightmare.

With that shocking news, I heard Desiree cry as she left the bathroom, leaving me feeling utterly alone, frightened, and furious at the cruel fate that had befallen us.

I paused staring at the blank wall as Desiree's words echoed in my mind. Grace—married off? It felt unreal, like a twisted dream I couldn't shake. I tried to focus on anything else, but my thoughts drifted back to the elevator incident.

The memory flashed vividly. That man, his presence looming and oppressive as we shared the cramped space of the elevator. He had a calm exterior, but something dark flickered behind his eyes. When he spoke about the girl who had been hurt for refusing to participate in the trials, I felt a shiver crawl down my spine. His voice had dripped with disdain for her weakness, an almost gleeful recounting of her punishment that made my stomach churn. What had happened to her?

I couldn't shake the nagging suspicion that it might have been Desiree. The thought tightened around my chest like a vice grip. Had she fought back and faced the consequences? The mere possibility made me sick with worry. She seemed to be strong-willed, but how far would she go?

The memory replayed itself—the way his hand bled, the bitterness of his voice. I bit down hard on my lip, desperate to hold back the swell of nausea rising within me. Did that girl have a family? Friends who would be devastated by her absence?

My thoughts spiraled further into despair as I considered what it all meant for us in this place—a system designed to crush spirits and silence dissenters. We were all just pawns in their game, but was there any way to fight back?

Suddenly, I heard a soft knock on the bathroom door. My heart raced as I glanced toward it; fear coursed through me like ice water. Who could it be? Desiree? Or perhaps someone wanting to deliver more bad news? Whatever it was, I knew one thing for certain: this nightmare was far from over.

I composed myself before stepping out of the bathroom, finding one of the girls waiting for my stall, my mind racing, and made my way back to my bed at the end of the row. I glanced over at Desiree, who still seemed to be in tears, her silhouette a haunting reminder of our grim situation.

I lay awake for at least an hour, seething at the thought of my sweet, innocent friend enduring the trials designed to break us. Eventually, my thoughts shifted to devising a plan to ensure I would never face those trials myself. Gradually, I began to think about the man who had been fixated on me since arriving here.

I concluded he must be unattractive, old, and self-absorbed. After all, no handsome man would seek anything less than an ideal beauty from a prestigious family. Surely, no young, strong leader would desire someone as defiant as I had been in the centers, someone who challenged the status quo at every turn. And no man with even a trace of kindness would grant a girl everything she desires, only to make her suffer repeatedly, to toy with her emotions like a puppet on a string. The thought of him filled me with a mix of anger and despair, as I tried to reconcile the idea of a man who could wield such power over a life as fragile as mine. Resolutely, I decided that I didn't want him. I didn't want to win. I didn't want any more remnants from the past. I was determined to make him give up on me.

My thoughts were only interrupted by Desiree's muffled sobs. Finally, gathering my composure, I walked over to her bed, climbed in, and wrapped my arms around her, offering what little comfort I could. "I'm so sorry for what you've endured. This place is hell, and I'm getting out of it," I whispered softly in her ear, hoping to instill a sense of hope amid the despair.

She stopped crying and turned to face me, her eyes shimmering with confusion and curiosity. "What do you mean?"

Chapter 14

Connor

Upon hearing the front door creak open and Jonathan step inside with the latest addition to our team, I exited my room and made my way down the grand staircase, the polished wood steps creaking softly underfoot. "Hello," I greeted Mia and Jonathan, a hint of warmth in my voice.

Mia's eyes widened in surprise as she glanced up at me, her expression a mix of apprehension, respect and fear that caught me off guard. "Sir," she replied, lowering her head like a soldier addressing a superior, which made me feel a uncomfortable mix of authority and unease. I wasn't used to this kind of deference, and it reminded me of the weight of my position.

Jonathan exhaled deeply, a sound I recognized well, indicating he was already reflecting on the daunting task before us: persuading her that this was a safe environment. "I'll handle monitoring the feed," he said, striding purposefully toward the hallway, his determination clear in every step. "I'm sure Shane could use a break." As he moved, I could see the flicker of resolve in his eyes, a reminder of the dedication we both shared to our cause.

As I approached, I noticed Mia stood frozen, her body tense with anxiety, like a deer caught in headlights. "Hey, please don't be scared of me," I said, striving to infuse my tone with as much gentleness as I could muster, hoping to pierce through the wall of apprehension surrounding her. "You are safe here, I promise." I wanted her to feel the sincerity of my words, to understand that this space was meant to provide refuge, not fear.

Finally, she met my gaze, her blue eyes filled with uncertainty and a hint of vulnerability that tugged at my heart. "I'm not sure if there's been a mistake; I'm not good enough to be cleaning all of this," she stammered, her voice trembling slightly. The self- doubt in her words struck a chord within me, and I couldn't hold back an involuntary chuckle, a mix of disbelief and empathy. How could she not see the strength she possessed?

"I have no clue how to run a household. Jonathan didn't have any idea how to be an assistant. And Shane, our electrician, is mediocre at best with electrical tasks," I reassured her, hoping to ease her worries. My voice was steady, but inside, I felt a storm of uncertainty. "You're here for my wife. She would be furious if I let anyone hurt you." I wanted her to understand the depth of my commitment, the fierce loyalty I felt towards Jessica.

"Your wife?" she asked, her brow furrowing in confusion, as if trying to piece together a puzzle that didn't quite fit. "I thought you were single."

I paused, the words hanging in the air like a fragile thread. Searching for the right words, I felt a slight blush creeping up my neck, warmth flooding my cheeks. "My future wife," I muttered, the weight of my feelings momentarily catching me off guard. It was a revelation that felt both exhilarating and terrifying, a promise I was desperate to keep. The thought of Jessica filled my mind, and I couldn't help but feel a surge of hope even amidst the uncertainty surrounding us.

Luckily, Carolynn, her dirty blonde hair flowing around her shoulders, interrupted us, bursting into the foyer with her lively spirit. "Hey Mia, you made it! I'm Carolynn," she exclaimed, wrapping her in a tight embrace before guiding her toward the living room. "I think you'll feel more *comfortable* if we talk in here."

Mia turned towards me, astonished, seeking my approval to go after her, and I nodded, wishing to alleviate the awkwardness. "Hey... she's the one who cooks, I just follow her orders," I chuckled, trailing behind Carolynn as Mia cautiously followed.

"Shhh," Shane hushed us as we stepped into the living area, his tone low and serious, a hint of urgency lacing his words. "What on earth is this girl doing?" He pointed at the screen, his expression filled with worry and confusion.

I stepped closer, curiosity piqued as I focused on the girl crawling toward Jessica's bed. Jessica lay sound asleep beneath the blankets, blissfully unaware of the unfolding scene, her chest rising and falling in a rhythmic pattern. The girl reached up, her small hand shaking Jessica gently, whispering something before crawling away toward the bathroom with an eerie, almost ghostly grace.

"Who is that?" I turned and stared at Shane, seeking answers in his furrowed brow and anxious eyes, trying to gauge how serious this situation might be.

"I don't know, Connor. She just appeared out of nowhere, and some of them swapped beds tonight," he replied, stifling a yawn that betrayed his fatigue and hinted at a long night. "Maybe I dozed off; I'm really sorry."

Jonathan cut in on the apology with a wave of his hand, dismissing the concern. "It's fine, man. We all zone out sometimes, and we were short-staffed tonight," he said, his voice steady, but I could sense his own unease lingering beneath the surface. I couldn't shake the feeling that something was off, and the girl's sudden appearance felt like a puzzle piece that didn't quite fit.

"He's right," I added, my voice steady, even as I felt the weight of the situation pressing down on me. "We'll just keep an eye on her; don't worry about it, Shane."

Carolynn cleared her throat, a playful glint sparkling in her soft blue eyes that teased the corners of her lips. "Stupid men, I think an introduction is necessary."

I chuckled at her lighthearted ribbing, the tension in the room easing just a bit. "Sorry, Mia. You've met Carolynn and Jonathan already, they are our cool and my assistant. But this strapping young lad, is Shane," I teased, gesturing toward him with a smirk.

"Hi," she stammered, her nervousness palpable as she shifted her weight from one foot to the other, her cheeks flushed. "Nice to meet you. Where's the rest of the staff?" Her voice trembled slightly, revealing the uncertainty that hung in the air like a thick fog.

Carolynn laughed, a melodic sound that warmed the room as she walked over, plopping down on Jonathan's lap and giving him a kiss that was both sweet and startling. "This is it, hun; it's a skeleton crew here. And we're more like family," she declared with a grin.

The two had become quite the couple in recent weeks, and I had given them my unnecessary, formal blessing a few days prior after stumbling upon them in a rather compromising situation in the pantry. The last thing I wanted was them getting frisky before my breakfast.

Mia's jaw dropped at the kiss, and I couldn't help but laugh at her wide-eyed reaction. "You'll discover things are quite different here. I want you all to feel comfortable and happy," I said, nodding toward the couple snuggled up on the couch. "And clearly, they are happy."

Shane gave Mia a reassuring pat on the back before wandering off to his room, leaving us in a comfortable, if chaotic, camaraderie that felt both familiar and warm. The kind of atmosphere that makes you forget about the outside world for just a moment.

Mia cautiously took a seat, her eyes glued to the screen, interest piqued as if she were about to witness something monumental. "Is this one of the centers?" she whispered, her tone a mix of curiosity and dread, the weight of the situation settling in the air around us. I could see the concern etched on her face, a reflection of the uncertainty we all felt.

I nodded slowly, feeling the weight of the moment pressing heavily on my chest. Just as I gathered my thoughts and prepared to speak, Jonathan burst in, his voice brimming with excitement that sliced through the thick tension in the air like a hot knife through butter. "She's moving!" he exclaimed, his enthusiasm infectious, momentarily lifting the cloud of apprehension that hung over us.

Mia stood abruptly, her eyes glued to the screen as she leaned closer, her heart racing in rhythm with the unfolding drama that seemed to envelop us all. "That's Jessica!" she exclaimed, recognition dawning on her like a sunrise breaking through the night, illuminating the shadows of worry that had cast a pall over our gathering.

Laughter erupted among us, a spontaneous outburst that sliced through the heaviness that had clung to the air just moments before. I couldn't help but smile at Mia's infectious enthusiasm; it was a reminder of the warmth and hope that still flickered amidst the uncertainty. "Yes, it is," I replied, my voice steady as I tried to anchor us back to the task at hand. "Now quiet down and sit so we can make sure she's okay." The urgency in my tone was meant to bring us back to focus, to shield us from the turmoil brewing just outside our small circle of camaraderie.

We intently watched as Jessica entered the bathroom, our collective breaths held in anticipation, each of us caught in our own web of concern and hope. Minutes felt like hours as we waited, and I could feel the curiosity in the room morphing into a palpable tension, a weight pressing down on us all. The silence was deafening, each tick of the clock amplifying our anxiety. When Desiree finally emerged, followed closely by Jessica, my heart raced with a mixture of relief and anxiety, the rush of emotions swirling inside me like a storm.

"So what was that?" I asked, my gaze darting between Jonathan and Carolynn, both of whom wore expressions of equal puzzlement. The atmosphere shifted again, the air thick with questions that hung unspoken, waiting for answers we weren't sure would come. I could sense the urgency in the room, the desperate craving for clarity amidst the chaos.

After a few moments of us staring at Jessica in bed, Mia broke the silence, her voice laced with confusion. "So, does anyone want to fill me in on what the hell is going on?" Her eyes flicked between us, searching for someone to make sense of the situation, a task that felt monumental given the circumstances.

Carolynn took the lead in explaining, her enthusiasm infectious even in this tense moment, with Jonathan and me chiming in, adding bits here and there, trying to piece together the puzzle. Each word we shared seemed to weave a thread of understanding through the confusion, but when we finally finished, Mia looked utterly baffled, her mind racing to catch up.

The bewilderment on her face was almost comical, yet it mirrored my own internal chaos. Eventually, she managed to respond, her voice tinged with an unexpected lightness, "I guess there really is a Knight in Shining Armor."

Chapter 15

Jessica

With hushed whispers under the covers while the others slept, it didn't take long for Desiree and I to come to a consensus that we wanted nothing to do with winning the center, and we were fully prepared to accept any consequences they might hand down. We had devised a scheme that we knew would create waves, and we were set to stir things up in a way that would leave an impression.

I quietly slipped away from her bed and returned to my own, careful not to disturb the fragile atmosphere of the room. An almost eerie silence enveloped us; everyone else was fast asleep, lost in their dreams. As I settled into my bed, I contemplated what I would confront if I went through with our plan. A twinge of fear gripped me, but beneath that, an exhilarating rush surged through me. I needed to seize control of my life for once, and this might be my last opportunity. I steeled myself to face whatever punishments awaited me, even if it meant risking everything. Deep down, I knew I absolutely refused to become a wife. I would not participate in raising children who could select their partners from centers to craft the life they desired. With my resolve firm, I drifted into my thoughts, eventually succumbing to sleep.

Around 4 a.m., the alarm rang as anticipated; it was time for the scavenger hunt. I quickly leaped out of bed, a rush of adrenaline coursing through me as I dashed to my vanity in search of a puzzle piece. My hand instinctively grabbed one, but to my surprise, there was no note this time. I stared at the piece in my palm, its edges cool against my skin, before inhaling deeply. This was the pivotal moment, the time to determine my destiny, and I could feel the weight of it pressing down on me.

I turned to see the flirtatious Meg beside me, looking lost and confused, her usual sparkle dimmed by uncertainty. She seemed like a shadow of her vibrant self, her golden curls falling slightly out of place. "Meg," I reached out and took her hands in mine, feeling the warmth of her skin against my own, a comfort amidst the chaos. "Are you alright?"

She nodded, tears welling in her eyes, glistening like trapped stars. "I'm just scared," she muttered, her voice barely above a whisper. "I'm not ready."

I smiled softly and embraced her, pressing our hands together and slipping the puzzle piece into her palm with a sense of urgency. "I'm ready; you need this more than I do," I whispered in her ear, my voice barely above a breath, before pulling away and racing toward the kitchen, my heart pounding with the thrill of the unknown.

I was the first to make it to the kitchen, my heart racing with anticipation as the smell of lingering coffee filled the air. I quickly discovered three puzzle pieces hidden in the microwave, coffee pot, and beneath the trash can, each one a small victory that made my spirit soar. As I rose from behind the kitchen island, feeling triumphant, I unexpectedly found myself face to face with Hope, a snooty girl I hadn't spoken to much. Her expression was a mixture of annoyance and disdain as she rolled her eyes, eyeing the puzzle pieces I clutched. "Well, it looks like you cleaned everything out in here," she groaned before turning on her heel and heading toward the bathroom, her disdain palpable and heavy in the air.

I jogged up next to her, my heart pounding in my chest, and slipped a puzzle piece into her hand, the unexpected gesture surprising even me. "One for you," I giggled into her ear, the thrill of the moment making me feel almost giddy, a spark of defiance igniting within me. The way her brows furrowed for a split second, as if she were trying to process my lightheartedness, made the risk worth it. I watched as her expression shifted, if only for a moment, before she pivoted away, and I made my way to the living room, eager for whatever awaited me next.

I managed to collect seven puzzle pieces throughout the competition, each one a testament to my strategy of distributing them as I went along. I did pretty well— one for Hope, two for Meg, two for Jake, and one for Harry. Each piece felt like a small victory, a step closer to something greater. However, I still had one left in my hand when I finished, just as they called us to the lockers, the finality of it hanging in the air like the last note of a song.

As I skipped into the bedroom, my mind racing with thoughts of the next challenge, I accidentally collided with a small, quiet blonde girl. The impact sent our puzzle pieces scattering across the floor, a colorful burst that looked like confetti from a celebration. "I'm so sorry," she immediately apologized, her voice shaky, the panic evident in her wide eyes as she watched the pieces tumble away.

"It's alright, that was my fault," I laughed, the sound light and airy as I bent down to gather them. I wanted her to know it was okay, that accidents happen. "What's your name again?"

She hurriedly collected the pieces, clearly anxious that I might take some that belonged to her. "Quinn," she whispered, glancing up at me, her expression a mix of apprehension and hope.

As I stood, I scooped up the remaining pieces, including the one I had left behind, and handed them to her with a smile. My heart swelled with a sense of camaraderie, a spark of connection in this seemingly chaotic environment. "Here you go, good luck," I said cheerfully, hoping to lift her spirits with my small gesture. I wanted her to feel included, to know that she wasn't alone in this daunting place filled with strangers and expectations. After a moment of shared understanding, I turned away, my mind buzzing with the possibilities of what lay ahead, the thrill of the competition still coursing through me like electricity.

I slipped into the bathroom, the cool tiles sending a shiver up my spine. The fluorescent lights flickered overhead, casting a harsh glow that revealed every imperfection. I glanced at the mirror and met my own reflection. My hair hung loosely, wild and unkempt, and my eyes sparkled with defiance.

Rebellion looks good on me, I thought as I examined my reflection closely. There was something liberating about the way I stood there—no longer cowering or conforming to anyone's expectations. My cheeks flushed with a mix of adrenaline and determination as I ran my fingers through my hair, tousling it even more. The image staring back felt like a stranger at first, but as I tilted my head slightly to one side, a sense of empowerment washed over me.

"Yeah," I whispered to myself, unable to suppress the smirk creeping across my lips. "This is me." The soft curve of my smile contrasted sharply with the uncertainty that had previously clouded my mind. In that moment, I embraced everything that had led me here: the frustration, the heartache, and now this rebellious streak sparking inside me.

I leaned closer to the mirror, examining the faint freckles scattered across my nose and cheeks. They reminded me of summer days spent outdoors with Mia and Grace, carefree moments when we believed we could conquer anything together. But those days felt distant now; this was no time for nostalgia. My reflection shifted from sweet innocence to someone determined to break free from constraints.

The urge to fight bubbled up within me like soda fizzing in a glass—quickening and effervescent. I squared my shoulders and stood tall in front of the mirror, adjusting my pink sundress just slightly to give it an edge rather than allowing it to hang limply against me.

"You're not going to let them break you," I told myself firmly, nodding at the person staring back with fierce resolve.

With one last look at myself—a girl poised on the brink of change—I stepped away from the mirror, ready to face whatever challenges awaited me outside those bathroom doors.

As I climbed into bed, I caught Desiree's eye as she passed by. She shrugged, and in that brief moment of eye contact, an unspoken understanding passed between us. I may have fulfilled our plan, but it seemed she had backed out, and I didn't hold it against her; I could only imagine the storm of punishment that awaited her should she choose to go through with it. I felt the weight of stares from around the bedroom, their scrutiny almost palpable, like a thick fog that enveloped me. The whispers of Meg and Jake floated through the air, their words a soft hum in the background, making it hard to concentrate. I couldn't help but smile as I pulled out my cell phone, seeking a moment of distraction.

With a flick of my thumb, I sent a text to my best friends, fully aware they would never see it: You won't believe what I just did. The excitement bubbled within me, a testament to my defiance and the uncertain future that lay ahead, a future that felt both exhilarating and terrifying all at once.

Chapter 16

Connor

I stared at the feed, frustration bubbling in my chest like a boiling pot ready to overflow as Jessica's defiance flickered across the screen. She had been my hope, the spark that could ignite change in this wretched system that suffocated so many. Now, she was throwing it all away, convinced she could tackle this alone, without any support from anyone else. If only she knew about the rest of us.

Jonathan leaned closer to the monitor, his brow furrowed in concern. "She can't be serious about this," he murmured, disbelief lacing his tone.

Mia crossed her arms defiantly, shaking her head as if trying to physically shake off the reality of the situation. "Why is she doing this? Does she really think she can fight back against them on her own?" Her voice was tinged with both confusion and anger.

Shane clenched his fists, his eyes narrowing at Jessica's image as if he could will her to change her mind with sheer force of will. "She's not just rebelling; she's putting herself in real danger," he stated, a protective instinct surging within him.

Carolynn sat rigid beside Jonathan, her face pale as worry twisted her features into a mask of dread. "They'll punish her for this! You know they will." Her voice trembled, and the depth of her fear hit me like a punch to the gut, intensifying the knot of anxiety tightening in my stomach.

Jonathan wrapped his arms around Carolynn, pulling her close to him. His touch was steady, a solid anchor in the storm of emotions swirling around us. "Hey, we'll figure something out," he reassured her, his voice firm and unwavering even as the weight of uncertainty pressed down on us. "We can't let them hurt her." I could see the determination in his eyes, and it sparked a flicker of hope within me, even as the dread of what lay ahead loomed large.

"Figure what out?" Mia snapped back at him, her voice rising with a frustration that felt nearly palpable in the air. "What if she doesn't listen? What if we can't change anything?" Each word cut through the charged atmosphere like a knife, laced with the bitterness of helplessness that had begun to seep into all of us. I could see her chest heaving with emotion, the tension in her shoulders betraying the turmoil brewing inside her. It was as if she was grappling with a storm of doubts, and I felt that same weight pressing down on me, threatening to drown us all in despair.

"We need to keep our heads clear," I interjected, forcing myself to rein in the anger bubbling just beneath the surface. It was crucial to focus on finding solutions rather than succumbing to the suffocating despair that threatened to envelop us all. "If she continues down this path, we'll lose her for good, and I can't bear the thought of that." The very notion sent a chill through me, and I could feel the weight of those words hanging heavy in the air. "I'll send another message"

Mia looked at me sharply, her eyes blazing with an intensity that matched the turmoil swirling around us. "You want to send her another note? That would just make things worse," she countered, her arms still crossed in defiance, as if she could physically block out any ideas she disagreed with. The fierce determination in her posture was commendable, but I could see that the frustration was also eating away at her.

"I'm just thinking—" I began, hoping to convey that my intentions were rooted in care, but I knew my voice sounded strained.

"No," Mia interrupted, shaking her head vehemently. "If she sees any notes from you, it'll only push her further away." The finality in her tone made it clear she was not open to discussion.

Mia's sharp gaze burned into me, and I felt the tension ripple through the air like a taut wire ready to snap.

Her outburst caught me off guard. I could see the flicker of uncertainty cross her face, and suddenly, the bravado melted away, leaving a vulnerability that tugged at my instincts to protect.

"I—" she stammered, her voice trembling slightly as she took a step back. "I didn't mean to push you. I just—" She ran a hand through her hair, her frustration morphing into something softer, more apologetic. "I care about Jessica, okay? She's one of my best friends."

I could feel the walls around us shift, the intensity of our earlier exchange fading into something more palpable—concern for Jessica binding us together in this moment of uncertainty. "I get that," I replied, my voice steadying as I locked eyes with Mia. "We all do. It's just..."

"Right," she cut in quickly, raising her hands in surrender as if to deflect any blame from herself. "I'm sorry for being so harsh."

Her sincerity caught me off guard again; it was refreshing to see her drop the bravado and let the concern shine through.

"I just want to make sure we don't lose her," Mia continued, her voice lowering as if afraid someone might overhear our conversation. "This is bigger than any of us."

I nodded slowly, appreciating her raw honesty. "It is bigger than us," I said quietly, absorbing her words as they hung in the air between us.

"I just thought maybe we could brainstorm or something?" she suggested tentatively, glancing at Jonathan and Carolynn for support but then quickly returning her focus to me.

"Sure," I agreed with a nod. "Let's find a way to reach out without pushing her further away."

Mia visibly relaxed at my response, relief washing over her features like sunlight breaking through clouds after a storm. But I could see that beneath it all, worry still etched lines across her brow.

"I don't want Jessica feeling alone in this," she added softly.

"We'll make sure she knows someone's here for her," I assured her, determination creeping back into my tone as I glanced around at Jonathan and Carolynn, who seemed ready to rally behind our cause too.

I ground my teeth together, frustration mounting as I ran a hand through my hair, feeling the weight of the world pressing down on me.

Shane glanced at Mia, then turned back to me with a spark of inspiration igniting in his eyes. "What if we find a way to give her an advantage? Something that keeps her safe but allows her to win?" His voice was filled with determination.

Jonathan nodded slowly, the gears in his mind beginning to turn as he contemplated the possibilities. "How do we do that? We can't be too obvious about it, or it'll backfire."

"Camilla," Mia suggested suddenly, her voice cutting through the tension. "She can get close to Jessica and knows how these competitions work inside out." There was a sense of urgency in her words, a glimmer of hope that perhaps this could work.

"That could work," I said, feeling a flicker of optimism creep back into my heart. Maybe we could reach her after all.

"She has connections," Shane added thoughtfully, his mind racing with the implications of that simple fact.

"Let's call Camilla," Jonathan said firmly, shifting into action mode, the determination evident in his posture.

As they prepared to reach out to Camilla, I felt my resolve strengthen, a renewed sense of purpose washing over me. We would do everything possible to ensure Jessica stayed safe and succeeded in this fight against the oppressive system that wanted nothing more than to crush her spirit and extinguish the light she brought into our lives.

I pulled up outside a modest house, its peeling paint and overgrown lawn a stark contrast to the polished facade of the world I inhabited. The cracked walkway seemed to whisper stories of neglect, while the faded shutters hung askew as if they were too tired to stand straight anymore. It was hard to believe that just beyond those weathered walls, someone lived a life so different from mine, a life perhaps filled with struggles I couldn't even begin to fathom. The air felt heavy with the weight of reality, reminding me that not everyone had the privilege of comfort and ease that I often took for granted. Camilla emerged from the door, her expression wary as she glanced around, taking in her surroundings with a mix of caution and anxiety before sliding into the passenger seat. The tension was palpable, and I could see fear etched deeply in her features, a silent testament to the weight of the world we were navigating.

"Drive," she instructed, her voice barely above a whisper, as if even the air around us was listening, holding its breath in anticipation.

I nodded, my heart racing, and took off, weaving through the side streets with a newfound sense of determination, keen to avoid any prying eyes that might be lurking in the shadows. Each turn heightened my sense of urgency, the weight of our mission pressing down on me like a heavy stone. I kept my focus firmly on the road ahead, but I couldn't help stealing glances at her from time to time.

Camilla fidgeted in her seat, her fingers tapping nervously against her thigh, a rhythmic dance of anxiety that mirrored my own turmoil. Her eyes darted frequently to the rearview mirror, as if she were convinced that someone was right behind us, poised to pounce at any moment.

"Camilla," I began, my voice slicing through the thick silence that hung between us like a dense fog, heavy and suffocating, wrapping us in a shroud of tension. "I need Jessica to win." The words felt like a weighty declaration, a promise that I was determined to keep, a vow forged from desperation and hope. But I could sense the gravity of the situation pressing down on us like an oppressive force, and I knew this was only the beginning of our challenges, a mere prelude to the trials that lay ahead.

She turned toward me sharply, her eyes widening with concern, a flicker of fear igniting in their depths, as if my words had awakened a reality she was desperate to avoid. "What are you talking about? You know how this works. She's at risk every moment she's there." Her voice trembled slightly, betraying her own anxiety, and I felt a pang of guilt for putting that fear in her eyes.

"I get that," I replied, my grip tightening on the steering wheel, knuckles going white as I fought against the rising tide of frustration that threatened to drown me. The thought of Jessica, vulnerable and exposed, fueled my determination. "But if we can give her an edge... We need to do everything we can to make sure she stays safe and comes out on top." My mind raced with strategies and possibilities, each one more urgent than the last, as I searched for a way to protect her in a world that seemed intent on tearing her down.

Her brow furrowed as she processed my words, a storm of emotions crossing her face that made her look both fierce and fragile at the same time. "And you think I can help?"

"Yes," I said firmly, conviction surging within me like a tidal wave. "You know the ins and outs of these competitions better than anyone else. You've seen how they operate, how they manipulate the players, weaving their webs of deceit and control."

Camilla bit her lip, uncertainty flickering across her face like a candle flame caught in a draft, struggling to stay lit in the gusts of doubt. "What's in it for me?"

I glanced at her, surprise mingling with curiosity at the unexpected turn of our conversation. "What do you want?" I asked, genuinely wanting to understand the depths of her desire.

She hesitated for a moment, her eyes searching for the right words, before finally speaking, the weight of her request palpable in the air between us. "My sister... Whatever happened to her? No one seems to know."

The gravity of her request settled between us like an unspoken pact, a bond forged in desperation and shared understanding that transcended the chaos surrounding us. It was as if the universe had conspired to bring us together, two souls adrift in a sea of uncertainty.

"If Jessica wins," I promised, my heart racing at the stakes now laid bare between us, "I'll find out what happened to your sister." The words felt heavy, but I meant them with every ounce of my being. I could almost feel the weight of her sister's absence pressing down on us both.

Her expression softened slightly, a flicker of hope shining through the apprehension that still lingered in her eyes, a quiet plea for trust that urged me to solidify our alliance.

"You're not just saying that?" she asked, searching my gaze for sincerity, a silent challenge that dared me to prove my commitment.

"I mean it," I assured her as we rounded another corner, my mind racing with strategies and possibilities that flooded my thoughts like a rushing river, the path ahead uncertain but filled with potential. Every twist and turn felt like a step deeper into the unknown, yet I was resolute.

Camilla nodded slowly, determination creeping back into her posture as we drove deeper into obscurity, both of us acutely aware that this was only the beginning of our alliance against a system designed to crush us all. An alliance born of necessity, but perhaps, in time, it could become something more—a force strong enough to challenge the very foundations of the world we lived in.

I turned to Camilla, curiosity gnawing at me like a persistent itch. "Why are you willing to risk everything just for an update about your sister?"

She glanced out the window, the scenery blurring past as if she were lost in thought. For a moment, silence enveloped us, thick and heavy with unspoken fears. I could see the way her jaw tightened, the muscles flexing beneath her skin as she weighed her response.

"My sister is actually my twin," she finally said, her voice low but steady. "She was born one minute late." A bitter smile tugged at her lips, a fleeting expression that hinted at a deeper pain. "Twins run in our family, and it's why I never got married. I didn't want to have children."

"Because of the Centers?" I prompted, trying to piece together the fragments of her story.

"Exactly." She nodded, her gaze still distant. "The Center Hunters are all unmarried. Their punishment for choosing not to marry and have children is this— taking second-borns from their families." She turned to face me fully, determination hardening her features. "We know most will end up living as servants or worse."

The weight of her words sank in like lead. Each syllable dripped with bitterness, each revelation a sharp stab of reality that cut through my privileged existence.

"So you've dedicated your life to this…this cycle?" I asked slowly, trying to grasp the depth of what she was saying.

"Yes," she said with quiet conviction. "It's not just about my sister anymore; it's about finally having the chance to break this cycle." Her eyes sparked with something fierce—rage or hope, perhaps both mingled together. "I refuse to sit idly by while lives are torn apart because of a law that shouldn't exist. I have been waiting for years for someone to care enough to just ask for my help for one of those children. You are the first person who has."

I felt a strange sense of admiration mixed with sympathy for her plight—a woman who had sacrificed so much to ensure she wouldn't have a child subject to this cruelty. But there was also fear swirling inside me; fear that this fight might cost us more than we could afford.

"Camilla…" I began but hesitated as the enormity of what lay ahead crashed down around us like an unrelenting tide.

"I'm not asking for sympathy," she interrupted softly but firmly, meeting my gaze head-on. "I'm asking you to let me help change things. Even if just for one girl."

Camilla leaned closer, her expression grave. "This job will be tougher than you realize, Mr. Dandin. The Center Liaisons are not pleased with Jessica's defiance. They're watching her every move, waiting for any sign of weakness to pounce."

I clenched my jaw, the reality of our situation settling heavily in my gut. "What do we do about it?"

She exhaled slowly, running a hand through her hair in frustration. "First, we need money—significant amounts. This isn't just about making a few calls; it's about buying influence and protection for Jessica. She'll need a powerful ally who can sway the Liaisons' decisions."

"Powerful how?" I asked, already feeling the pressure of what lay ahead. My family had resources, but this was an entirely different game.

"We'll need someone well-connected, someone who can navigate this twisted world without raising suspicion." Camilla's gaze held mine, intensity flickering in her eyes. "If we approach the wrong person or go about it carelessly, it could backfire catastrophically."

"Do you have anyone in mind?" The urgency gripped me tighter.

Camilla turned her gaze out the window, deep in thought, the cityscape blurring past us. "Do you know the future governor, Theo George?" she asked, her voice steady but laced with a hint of hope that seemed to resonate within the confines of the car.

I felt a jolt at the mention of his name. Theo George was a figure that loomed large in our society— handsome, charismatic, and seemingly destined for greatness. The whispers of his impending rise to power echoed everywhere, and everyone talked about him as if he were some kind of savior in waiting. I'd never crossed paths with him, though. "I've heard of him," I admitted, gripping the steering wheel a little tighter, the tension coiling in my shoulders. "But why do you think he would be trustworthy?"

Her eyes flickered back to me, intense and unwavering, the weight of her gaze grounding me. "I can't say for certain," she replied, frustration evident in her tone, her fingers tapping restlessly against the leather seat. "But I have reason to believe he's pulled strings in a center before. He might be willing to do it again." She leaned forward slightly, as if trying to gauge my reaction, her urgency palpable.

"Pulled strings?" My skepticism slipped through despite my efforts to mask it. The idea that someone like Theo George would risk his birthright political career to intervene on behalf of someone like Jessica seemed far-fetched at best, a notion that felt almost reckless to entertain.

"Yes," she insisted, passion igniting her words as her voice rose slightly. "There are whispers about his involvement in past decisions—favors traded under the table to protect specific individuals from elimination or harsh punishments." The implications of her words hung in the air, heavy with potential.

My mind raced as I weighed her claims against everything I knew about Theo George. He had the kind of reputation that made people take notice, especially among those who craved power and influence. But would he risk everything for a girl he didn't know? "And what makes you think he'd care about her?" The question slipped out, a mix of disbelief and a desperate hope for clarity.

Camilla paused for a moment, biting her lip as if choosing her next words carefully, the tension in the car thickening. "I can't guarantee anything," she finally said, frustration tinged with determination coloring her voice, each word measured yet fervent. "But if anyone could empathize with our situation— understand what it means to fight against an oppressive system—it would be him."

The thought lingered in my mind like a beacon of possibility amidst the encroaching darkness surrounding us, an ember of hope in a world that felt increasingly bleak.

"Alright," I said slowly, weighing my options and realizing we had little choice but to reach out to him. The urgency of our predicament pressed against my chest, and I knew we had to act.

"I'll contact Theo myself," Camilla stated firmly, determination etched into her features as we drove deeper into uncertainty together, the road ahead stretching out like an uncharted territory, fraught with both peril and promise.

Chapter 17

Jessica

The atmosphere buzzed with anticipation as Mrs. Smith strolled in, her heels clicking against the floor like a metronome counting down to the moment of truth. Each click reverberated in my chest, amplifying the tension that hung thick in the air.

"Listen up, everyone!" she called, her voice slicing through the murmur of conversations like a knife through butter. "It's time to announce the winners of this morning's competition!"

I felt my heart race, a frantic drumbeat that matched the growing unease around me, as she unfolded a piece of paper with deliberate slowness. Quinn stood beside me, her fingers fidgeting with the hem of her shirt, betraying her own anxiety. I wished I could offer her some comfort, but I was too wrapped up in my own nerves.

"Today, we celebrate two winners: the participant with the most puzzle pieces and the one with the least!" She paused for dramatic effect, scanning our faces as if searching for the right reaction before continuing.

A ripple of tension and confusion coursed through the group; it seemed like almost everyone knew this wasn't normal. It was always the person with the most, never the least. The absurdity of it all twisted in my stomach.

"The first winner," she said, grinning broadly, "with an impressive haul of pieces… Quinn!"

"And for those who collected fewer pieces," she continued, "the other winner is Jessica! You're both safe from leaving."

Quinn gasped beside me, her eyes wide with surprise. We exchanged quick smiles, but I was stunned; I didn't want to win. I wanted out of this mess, out of these competitions that felt more like traps than games.

"Now for those who need to be concerned," Mrs. Smith's tone shifted, her smile fading into something more serious. "The bottom five are Annie, Aaron, Jake, Meg, and Harry." Each name hung in the air like a heavy cloud, darkening the mood around us.

Annie and Aaron? I hadn't really talked to them before— always observing them quietly from a distance while they huddled together, whispering secrets amidst the chaos. A pang of guilt hit me for not reaching out sooner; their shared silence spoke volumes about their bond, a connection forged in quiet understanding.

Mrs. Smith continued on about disciplinary actions or whatever nonsense followed these announcements, but I hardly heard it over the thundering in my chest and the gnawing worry that crept into my mind.

With a dismissive wave of her hand and a half- hearted murmur about wishing she could decide discipline herself, Mrs. Smith turned on her heel and left as quickly as she'd come, leaving an uneasy silence in her wake.

My gaze drifted toward Annie and Aaron. They exchanged looks filled with worry, their expressions twisting my insides further. What had they been through? Did they share my eagerness to be cut loose, or was it just fear that bound them to this place like chains? I wished I could understand their struggle, to bridge the gap that had formed between us without my even realizing it.

As the tension finally dissolved, we all gravitated toward the kitchen, a collective sigh of relief escaping our lips like a long-held breath. The comforting aroma of melting cheese and grilled tortillas filled the air, wrapping around us like a warm blanket. Quinn took charge, her hands deftly flipping quesadillas on the stovetop with an ease that surprised me. I leaned against the counter, watching her with a mix of admiration and curiosity.

"Who knew you were such a culinary genius?" I teased, trying to inject a bit of levity into our atmosphere, hoping to lighten the mood that had clung to us just moments before.

Quinn chuckled, her cheeks turning a shade pinker under the weight of the compliment. "It's not rocket science. Just don't burn it," she replied with a playful grin that momentarily chased away the shadows lurking in our minds.

Once lunch was ready, we settled around the kitchen island, a sense of eagerness bubbling up within us as we anticipated something warm and comforting to fill our bellies. As we dug into our food, I could see Meg leaning in closer, her eyes sparkling with mischief, ready to bring some life back into our gathering.

"Okay, let's share some family stories. I mean, we're all in this mess together. Might as well get to know each other better," she suggested, her voice animated and inviting.

I took a bite of my quesadilla, the flavors dancing on my tongue, and nodded in agreement. It felt like a good idea—like a thread connecting us through our shared experiences, weaving a tapestry of camaraderie in this unsettling time. Quinn spoke first, her voice soft yet steady.

"My parents... tried to keep me hidden," she began slowly, her tone almost wavering as the memories surfaced. "I was born at home and never allowed outside for most of my childhood. Until I was fifteen when neighbor reported us because she saw me in the backyard a few times." She paused, letting the weight of her words sink in, the silence wrapping around us like a shroud. "They thought they could protect me from all this... But look where I ended up."

The heaviness of her confession lingered in the air; I could see reflections of my own fears flickering in her eyes, mirroring the uncertainty we all felt.

"I miss my siblings," Jake chimed in next, his expression serious yet gentle. "We used to play football every weekend before…" His voice trailed off into a somber silence, the loss palpable in his words.

"Same here," Harry added quickly, his tone earnest. "My little sister is just two; she doesn't understand any of this yet. She won't even remember who I am." The sadness in his voice tugged at my heart, a reminder of the innocence being stripped away from us all.

Desiree glanced around at us, her gaze softening as she shared her truth. "My parents were always pretty supportive, but they were scared too—always trying to shield me from the reality of what's happening out here." Her admission hung in the air, a quiet testament to the struggles we each faced.

I swallowed hard, feeling tears prick at my eyes, stinging with the weight of our shared burdens. It felt good to share that weight, even just a little bit, as we leaned on each other in this moment of vulnerability.

Meg broke into our somber moment with a bright grin. "Well, my parents run a restaurant! I used to serve tables but they wanted me to be a chef." She laughed lightly, shaking her head as if recalling an amusing memory. "Let's just say that didn't go well— I'm terrible at cooking!" Her smile faded slightly as she continued more seriously, "But it's tough now; my younger sister will have to come here too someday since they never had a boy."

As Meg spoke about her family's struggles and the fact her father would be forced to continue working the restaurant until he died just because he never produced a male heir, an unexpected warmth settled within me—a flicker of camaraderie amidst the horror surrounding us all.

I leaned in closer, intrigued by the quiet girl sitting across from me who had started fidgeting nervously. Annie's eyes flickered with a mixture of fear and determination as she finally found the courage to speak up.

"Aaron is my little brother," she said, her voice barely above a whisper, almost swallowed by the weight of the room. "I hadn't seen him for two years." The words hung in the air like a heavy fog, thick with unspoken pain and longing, leaving a palpable silence in their wake.

"How is that even possible?" I blurted out, unable to contain my curiosity any longer. The question slipped from my lips, fueled by a mix of disbelief and concern. I felt the weight of everyone else's eyes on her, just as curious and equally desperate to understand the depths of her situation.

Annie hesitated, biting her lip as if weighing how much to reveal, her expression shifting between vulnerability and guardedness. "I've been bounced around between centers and holding facilities for years," she admitted, frustration seeping into her tone like a dark ink stain. "I don't even know why. It's driving me insane." The rawness of her words sliced through me, leaving a chill running down my spine. The thought of being shifted like a pawn in some cruel game unsettled me deeply, a grim shadow creeping into my mind.

Aaron nodded solemnly beside her, his brown eyes darkening with intensity, a storm brewing behind them. "Our father… he's an evil and powerful man," he said, his voice trembling slightly but unwavering, as if he were drawing strength from the very core of his being. "They just keep having more children, fully aware that we'll be sent away to these places."

"More kids?" My mind raced as I tried to process this startling revelation. The idea of more younger siblings —innocent children who might also end up trapped in this twisted system—sent a wave of nausea through me.

"Yes," Aaron continued, glancing at Annie with a look that held a shared history of pain before looking down at his hands clenched tightly on the table, as if he were trying to anchor himself to reality. "He wants to control us, use us like tools for whatever purpose he has in mind. They had a son and a daughter, but still decided to have Annie, then me, followed by our sisters Alice and Asia. We've never even met the older two, and my memories of my mother are hazy at best. The staff essentially raised us spare kids. Dad would stop in to make sure we were still alive."

Annie sighed heavily, the sound escaping her like a deflated balloon. "Before I left, I would hear whispers from the staff… mentioning something about how I he would keep us in pairs, that Aaron and I would be in a Center together" she confessed, each word weighted with bitterness and disbelief, as if the truth was a bitter pill she had to swallow. "And that we would depart as a pair. Dispatched to some sort of breeding initiative designed to study & compare our DNA, ensuring they acquire only the finest characteristics from each of us, and then combine us with the extras from other influential families to produce the ideal first-borns to guide our nation." The implications of her words struck me like a lightning bolt, sending shockwaves through my chest. My heart sank at the horror of it all, spiraling into a tangled web of manipulation and despair that felt all too real.

"Breeding initiative?" Meg echoed incredulously from across the table, her voice laced with disbelief and horror, as if she couldn't quite grasp the depths of what Annie had just shared.

"Yeah," Aaron said quietly but firmly, the conviction in his voice a stark contrast to the sickening reality they faced. "It's sickening, we were created to be guinea pigs."

As their harrowing stories unfolded like a dark tapestry before us, I couldn't help but feel a sense of solidarity forming among us—a bond forged through shared anguish and unrelenting determination against the circumstances that sought to tear us apart. In that moment, amidst the despair, I sensed a flicker of hope igniting within me, a quiet promise that we would fight together against the darkness threatening to engulf us.

The anger in the room bubbled up like a pot about to boil over. I could see it in everyone's eyes, the way they clenched their jaws and tightened their fists. It was a fire igniting, fueled by the weight of our shared truths.

"We can't keep letting them control us like this!" Harry exclaimed, his voice rising above the simmering tension. "What's the point of participating in these twisted games? We're not puppets for their entertainment!"

"Exactly!" Meg jumped in, her cheeks flushed with indignation. "They expect us to just roll over and play nice while they plan our futures without even asking us what we want. No more!"

Desiree's face shone with determination as she leaned forward, her words punctuated with fervor. "We should refuse to participate altogether! If enough of us stand together, maybe we can actually make a difference."

As those words hung in the air, I felt my heart race with excitement and fear alike. What if we really did band together? The thought felt dangerous yet liberating, a flicker of hope igniting against the oppressive gloom surrounding us.

But just as that spark caught fire, blaring announcements echoed through the center, cutting through our conversation like a sharp knife.

"Attention participants: discussing illegal activities is considered treasonous behavior," a mechanical voice warned from the loudspeakers overhead. "All participants must cease discussions immediately and return to acceptable conversation."

I glanced around at these new friends; confusion mixed with frustration clouded their faces. My pulse quickened as I pushed aside that looming threat in my mind. Who were they to dictate what we could or couldn't talk about?

Ignoring the speaker's warning felt both reckless and thrilling. Desiree shot me a look filled with resolve. "We can't let them intimidate us into silence," she urged fiercely. "This is our chance to fight back."

Harry nodded vigorously, leaning closer as if forming an unbreakable bond between us in that moment. "We can't let them win! If we stay silent now, what's next? They'll take everything from us!"

I swallowed hard, each word resonating deep within me, stirring something I hadn't dared acknowledge before—the courage to stand up against this madness.

The announcements blared on repetitively above us, drowning out our voices yet failing to snuff out the fire ignited by our anger and defiance. I gripped the edge of the counter tightly, feeling a surge of adrenaline coursing through my veins as I prepared to join Desiree and continue this fight for our freedom amidst the chaos surrounding us.

A new announcement blared through the air, jolting me from my thoughts. "Attention: The live feeds have been disabled." A heavy silence enveloped us for a fleeting moment, an announcement that felt almost surreal. Then, without warning, a loud siren pierced the stillness, slicing through the tension like a knife. The exterior door crashed open, sending a rush of wind and panic swirling into the room, and I instinctively recoiled, my heart racing at the sudden chaos that erupted around us.

Chapter 18

Connor

Watching the feed, I felt my heart race, thudding in my chest as the announcer's voice echoed through the room with an electrifying energy. "Jessica! The winner of today's challenge!"

A wave of relief washed over me, so strong it felt like I could finally breathe again. A grin stretched across my face, one I couldn't contain. Camilla had pulled it off. Somehow, she had managed to navigate the treacherous waters of the rules and change them in our favor.

Mia leaned back on the couch, her expression a delightful mix of disbelief and joy. "I can't believe it! She did it!"

Her enthusiasm was infectious, and I couldn't help but feel the same thrill coursing through my veins.

Shane nodded, his eyes glued to the screen in admiration. "She's got guts, that one." His respect for Jessica was evident, and I felt a swell of pride for her as well.

I held back the urge to bring up Theo Dandin's role in this unexpected twist of fate. It wasn't the right time for that discussion—not yet, anyway. We needed to savor this moment of victory before diving into the complexities of what had transpired.

Mia turned her gaze toward me, a teasing smile dancing on her lips. "You know, Connor, this mansion is great and all, but it looks like a bachelor pad. You might want to rethink your decorating choices."

"Hey," I protested, crossing my arms defensively, though I couldn't help but chuckle at her playful jab. "It has character."

"It needs more than character." She chuckled, shaking her head in mock disapproval. "Get yourself a female assistant to run this place properly. Maybe someone with a little flair?"

Shane snorted at that idea, but Mia pressed on, clearly enjoying the banter.

"And definitely hire a landscaper before the weeds take over," she added, adopting a mock serious tone that made me laugh even harder.

I shot them both an incredulous look, half-amused and half-exasperated. "Okay, okay. Let's make a list of staff we need." I paused, contemplating the reality of what we truly needed to transform this house from just an oversized box into a place that felt like home.

"Dot from my center could be a great assistant," Shane suggested, his brow furrowing in thought as he considered the possibilities.

Mia raised an eyebrow at him, her curiosity piqued. "Oh really? Is there something you're not telling us?"

Shane shrugged, but the sheepish grin breaking through his facade was a dead giveaway, fueling our teasing even more.

"She'd bring some charm to this place," he insisted defensively, though the hint of embarrassment in his tone was unmistakable. It was amusing to see him flustered, a stark contrast to his usual confident demeanor.

Mia and I exchanged glances, the unspoken camaraderie between us amplifying the moment, before we burst into laughter at Shane's expense. It felt good to share this lightheartedness, to let our worries about the future dissipate, if only for a few moments.

"Looks like someone has a crush!" I teased, leaning into the lighthearted atmosphere that surrounded us. It felt good to break free from the weight of our worries, even if just for a moment.

Shane rolled his eyes dramatically, but a smile crept onto his face despite our playful ribbing. It was hard to resist poking fun at him when he got all flustered like this.

"I'm just saying she's capable," he insisted, his tone defensive but his eyes betraying him. We could see right through his facade, the way he lit up at the thought of her.

As we settled into our easy banter, the sound of our laughter filled the room, pushing away the shadows that often threatened to close in on us. We brainstormed more ideas for staff, throwing out suggestions that danced in the air like confetti.

Meanwhile, Jessica's center in the background, they were making lunch and laughing—a shimmering reminder of hope amidst the chaos of our lives. It brought a warmth to my chest, a flicker of optimism that we could rally together, that we could somehow carve out a space for ourselves in this tumultuous world.

The laughter faded abruptly as the loudspeaker blared through the feed, drowning out our lightheartedness like a sudden storm sweeping in to shatter a peaceful day.

"Attention," the robotic voice droned, sending an icy chill down my spine that felt all too familiar in these moments of dread.

I shot a glance at Mia, her eyes widening in alarm, reflecting the unease that gripped us all. She stood abruptly, her earlier joy replaced by a tense energy that filled the room like static electricity.

"What now?" she muttered, crossing her arms tightly across her chest as if trying to shield herself from the impending announcement.

Shane's brow furrowed, his usual bravado evaporating into thin air like mist under the sun. "This can't be good," he said, his voice low and strained as he clenched his fists at his sides, a sign of his rising anxiety.

The chatter in the room fell to a hush as we strained to hear every word that followed, our breaths caught in our throats. My heart raced with dread; I had seen enough chaos in these centers to know that "important announcements" often meant trouble was brewing on the horizon.

The feed flickered, and for a fleeting moment, I hoped it was just a technical glitch, a harmless interruption in our lives. But the announcement continued, relentless.

"Attention…"

Mia turned toward me, her face pale as if the life had drained from her. "What do you think they mean?" she asked, her voice trembling slightly.

"I don't know," I admitted, frustration creeping into my voice. "They won't stop talking, and we can't hear the announcement clearly." Anxiety coiled tighter within me, making it hard to breathe.

Shane stepped closer to us, his eyes darting around the room like a trapped animal searching for an escape. "What if they're changing something? What if Jessica—"

"Stop," I cut him off sharply, feeling the panic rising within me like a tidal wave threatening to crash over. "We can't jump to conclusions."

But it was too late; our minds spiraled into chaos with every word that echoed through the speakers, each syllable a cold reminder of the uncertainty we faced.

Suddenly, Jonathan and Carolynn burst into the room from the kitchen, their faces painted with confusion that mirrored our own.

"What's going on?" Jonathan asked, his brow furrowed as he looked between us, searching for answers in our anxious expressions.

I could barely respond before another blaring announcement interrupted us, shattering what little calm remained.

"Attention: The live feeds have been disabled."

My stomach dropped as I met Shane's eyes—fear mirrored in both of us, a silent acknowledgment of the storm brewing just out of sight.

"What does that even mean?" Carolynn breathed out, her voice barely above a whisper.

"Something's gone wrong," Mia said shakily, her words tumbling out in a rush of dread.

Before anyone could say another word, the screen went black, the silence that followed suffocating us like a heavy fog.

A suffocating silence enveloped us as reality sank in like cold water over our heads, leaving us gasping for answers. We stood there, frozen in disbelief and uncertainty, wondering what lay ahead or where Jessica was right now, isolated from us without any visual connection to her world.

My heart raced as the announcement hung in the air, heavy with implications that threatened to suffocate me. I couldn't sit idle any longer; the weight of inaction pressed down on my chest. I pulled out my phone, my hands trembling slightly as I dialed Camilla's number, the urgency of the moment coursing through my veins.

The line connected, but instead of her usual calm demeanor that I relied on, a chaotic noise erupted from the other end, sending a jolt of fear through me.

"Let me in! You can't keep me out of there!" Camilla screamed, her voice sharp and frantic, cutting through the static like a knife.

I pressed the phone closer to my ear, straining to make sense of the clamor around her, the background noise a cacophony of shouting and confusion.

"I don't care what your orders are!" she shouted again, her

frustration palpable as muffled voices responded to her, but their words were indistinct, lost in the turmoil.

"Camilla!" I shouted into the phone, desperation creeping into my voice like a shadow I couldn't shake. "What's happening?"

She paused, and I could almost hear her taking sharp breaths, her anxiety mirroring my own. "Connor, I'm doing everything I can! They won't let any Center Hunters in! The feeds are down; it's complete chaos."

Panic bubbled within me like a boiling pot about to overflow, threatening to spill over and consume my thoughts. "What do you mean chaos? Is Jessica—"

"They're saying everyone inside has been found guilty of treason," she cut in sharply, her tone clipped, each word a hammer striking against my resolve. "They've sent in guards with Mrs. Smith to bring order."

I swallowed hard at the mention of treason, the impact of her words tightening my chest like a vice. The thought of Jessica caught up in something so perilous sent icy tendrils of fear curling around my heart.

"Is she okay? Are you sure?" My voice barely held steady, quaking with concern.

"Connor, listen," she said urgently, each word a lifeline thrown into turbulent waters. "I can't get through to anyone inside right now. The guards are taking control of the situation and shutting everything down."

"Shutting it down? What does that mean?" I gripped the phone tighter, feeling a wave of helplessness wash over me, threatening to pull me under.

"It means we're running out of time," Camilla replied sharply, her urgency a stark reminder of the gravity of our situation. "I'll keep trying to find a way in or get information from someone, but we might just need to wait this out. She might be on her own for this one."

I paced back and forth in my room, the familiar surroundings suddenly feeling constricting, as my mind raced through a whirlwind of options—anything, anything at all that could help Jessica escape this nightmare unfolding around her. Each step was a futile attempt to shake off the dread that clung to me like a second skin.

Chapter 19

Jessica

Chaos erupts as the doors fly open, and men with cattle prods rush in, their harsh commands filling the room like a thunderstorm. The guys scream at us to keep quiet and move towards the courtyard, their voices echoing off the cold, sterile walls. Meg, ever the inspired rebel, shouts back with a fiery defiance that reverberates through the air, only to be met with a painful jolt from one of the prods. The sharp crackle sends a chill down my spine, and within an instant, we fall silent, paralyzed by fear and the chilling realization of what we're facing. Scared to make any sudden movements, we brace ourselves as Mrs. Smith enters the center, her presence commanding and oppressive. Her voice, dripping with contempt and authority, accuses us all of treason as if we're nothing more than traitors in her grand narrative.

We're herded roughly into the courtyard, the summer sun beating down on us like a punishment, its rays feeling like a spotlight exposing our vulnerabilities. Mrs. Smith stands before us, a figure of cold detachment, her eyes scanning us with a predatory gaze as she calls out the names of the bottom five: Annie, Aaron, Jake, Meg, and Harry. My heart aches for my friends, each name feeling like a dagger to my chest. I know this isn't personal for Mrs. Smith, but the way she relishes in our despair makes it hard to believe she feels any semblance of humanity.

They are ordered to undress and get into the pool, the command echoing ominously in the stillness of the courtyard. Slowly, they begin to remove their clothes, each piece falling away like the last vestiges of their dignity. The guards prod them impatiently when they hesitate, their eyes glinting with a cruel thrill at the show of power. I watch, feeling a tumultuous mix of anger and helplessness, as my friends are stripped of everything that makes them who they are. Annie's frail body shakes, a tremor of fear, while Aaron's usually confident stance falters, a testament to the weight of the moment as they inch towards the pool. Jake's muscles tense, ready for a fight that he knows he can't win, and Meg's eyes flash with defiance, a spark of rebellion against the oppressive atmosphere. Harry stands tall, trying to project strength despite the threat looming over them, his bravado a thin shield against the reality surrounding us.

This isn't fair. I clench my fists so tightly that my nails dig into my palms, fearing my own nakedness under my clothes, haunted by the memories of humiliation that come flooding back—standing on display, even clothed, as a child, feeling the weight of judgment in every glance. But even in the depths of my dread, I refuse to let Mrs. Smith see my fear. I lift my chin, summoning every ounce of strength I possess, and meet her gaze with unwavering resolve. It is a silent promise that I will not back down, that I will fight for my friends, for all of us, even if it means standing against the very forces that seek to break us.

I felt the walls closing in around us as Desiree, Quinn, and I were corralled into a corner, the oppressive weight of Mrs. Smith's gaze pressing down like a physical force. My heart raced as I watched the pool shimmer under the harsh sun, reflecting the reality of what was happening. "Let me take Annie's place," Desiree pleaded, her voice trembling yet defiant. Her desperation cut through the air, raw and vulnerable. I wanted to scream that it wasn't right—that none of this was right—but I knew better than to voice my thoughts.

Desiree's voice rang out, a plea tinged with desperation. "Let me take Annie's place!" Her words hung in the air, charged with raw emotion. The tension crackled like electricity, and I could feel everyone holding their breath.

A guard turned sharply at her outburst, eyes narrowing like a hawk spotting its prey. Before I could even process the shift in atmosphere, he lunged toward Desiree, prodding her roughly with the end of his cattle prod.

"Shut your mouth, girl!" he barked, his voice slicing through the heavy silence like a knife. Desiree stumbled back, a gasp escaping her lips as the jolt coursed through her.

"No!" I shouted before I could stop myself. Panic surged through my veins as I watched Desiree's expression twist from defiance to shock and pain. My heart raced; fear gripped me like a vice.

"Shut it!" another guard warned me, advancing toward my side as if ready to inflict punishment on anyone who dared to speak up. My throat tightened, and I fought against the urge to shrink back under his gaze.

Desiree straightened herself despite the shock still dancing across her features. "You can't do this!" she shouted again, louder now, igniting my own spirit of rebellion. The guard sneered at her resolve but didn't respond immediately; he just stood there like a mountain of authority and intimidation. But I saw it—the flicker of uncertainty in his eyes when faced with someone unyielding. It gave me hope for just a moment.

As we stood there in our corner, I felt our small group tightening together like an unbreakable chain—my pulse quickening with every heartbeat. There was strength in unity, even in this dark place.

Then Mrs. Smith stepped forward again, her heels clicking ominously against the concrete as she glared down at us from her position of power. "You all need to learn your place," she declared coldly. Her words dripped with contempt as if she found our spirit amusing but utterly unacceptable.

I couldn't let them break us—especially not Desiree. She had risked everything for Annie; we couldn't just stand by and watch as they tore apart our bonds one by one. As I searched for words that would somehow express my fury and fear without sealing our fate further, the reality of what was happening sank deep into my bones.

Yet, something changed inside me—a flame kindled by our shared battle against tyranny and trepidation— and in that moment, it became essential to resist this monstrous system intent on devouring us entirely. Just as I was about to voice my thoughts, the two guards hovering over Desiree and me simultaneously jabbed us in the ribs with their prods, forcing us to collapse onto our knees in agony, that would leave a permanent physical reminder.

Mrs. Smith merely raised an eyebrow, her lips curling into a disdainful smile as she opened a shading umbrella for herself and settled into a chair with an air of superiority. The moment felt surreal, like we were characters in some twisted play where our lives hung in the balance for her amusement.

"Swim to the middle of the deep end," she commanded, her voice smooth but laced with menace. "If you touch the edge or go where you can stand, you'll be prodded back."

The words echoed in my mind as if they were carved into stone. My pulse quickened with each heartbeat as I tried to grasp the enormity of what she just declared. Drowning? Someone would die today? It was unthinkable—yet here we were.

A sharp gasp escaped Quinn's lips beside me, her eyes wide with disbelief. "You can't be serious!" she blurted out.

Mrs. Smith simply shrugged, unfazed by our horror. "One person will die today," she stated matter-of-factly, glancing at our friends in the pool who were now eyeing each other nervously. "The others will leave this center immediately after."

My stomach churned at her words—so clinical, so devoid of humanity. Annie's frightened face swam in my mind as I recalled how brave she'd been through all this; it wasn't fair that someone like her could lose her brother while Mrs. Smith lounged in comfort.

"Desiree!" I hissed, trying to catch her attention before it was too late. "Don't—"

Yet it was unfolding before my eyes; Desiree surged ahead boldly, willing to gamble everything for Annie and Aaron while dread gnawed at my stomach like a wild beast eager to escape its confinement. The guard slammed her against the wall, which ultimately subdued her.

The water lapped around them, each ripple echoing the tension that hung in the air like a heavy fog, thick and suffocating. I waited in the corner of the pool deck alongside Quinn and Desiree, our bodies tense as we watched the scene unfold before us, each moment twisting the pit in my stomach tighter. Annie and Aaron floated close to each other, their expressions locked in a silent conversation, words trapped behind clenched jaws, as if the very act of speaking could shatter the fragile bubble of hope that surrounded them. Fear radiated from them like heat from a flame; I could feel it as surely as they felt the cold water against their skin, a stark reminder of the perilous situation we were all entangled in.

Nearby, Jake, Harry, and Meg formed a little circle, moving together in an unspoken agreement that spoke volumes. Their eyes darted around as they scanned the pool's perimeter, taking stock of our disarray while keeping their breaths steady, each one a calculated effort to maintain calm in the face of uncertainty. But even through their outwardly calm exteriors, I noticed the strain creeping into their movements, the way their shoulders hiked up just a little too high, the slight tremor in their hands as they adjusted their positions.

A clock on the wall ticked away the seconds, the sound reverberating through my mind like a countdown to an inevitable conclusion. It felt surreal to watch the minutes pass by—five minutes… ten minutes… I lost track of how long they'd been treading water when it hit one hour. Still, they swam on, muscles aching but survival instinct driving them forward, a testament to their resilience against the overwhelming odds stacked against us.

I glanced over at Harry; his brow glistened with sweat mixed with pool water, a testament to the effort he was pouring into each stroke. He struggled to keep his chin above the surface now, panting lightly between strokes, his breath coming in ragged gasps. Each inhale seemed heavier than the last as he forced himself to stay afloat beside Jake and Meg, the weight of their situation pressing down on all of us.

"Come on, Harry," I whispered under my breath, wishing my words could reach him through this suffocating silence that wrapped around us like a shroud. He nodded slightly but didn't meet my eyes— his focus entirely on staying buoyant, on fighting against the tide of despair that threatened to engulf him.

At ninety minutes in, the original guards began to shift out, their replacements stepping forward with an air of confidence that sent a chill down my spine. Mrs. Smith sauntered over to greet them, her familiar disdainful smile stretching across her face like a mask, hiding whatever malevolence lurked beneath.

"Thank you for standing out here," she drawled sweetly to the departing guards, her tone dripping with false sympathy as they retreated from their posts in the blistering sun, leaving us to the mercy of this new wave of enforcers.

Just then, a pair of guards approached our little group in the corner, carrying three water bottles—an unexpected sight amidst this madness. They handed them off to Desiree, Quinn, and me without ceremony, as though they were merely tossing scraps to starving animals. My fingers trembled slightly as I grasped one of those precious bottles; it felt heavy yet life-giving all at once, a small token of relief in the midst of our struggle.

"Don't drink too fast," one guard warned dryly, his eyes glinting with a mix of amusement and indifference before turning back toward his colleagues with a smirk that made my stomach churn.

I exchanged worried glances with Desiree and Quinn, the unspoken fear mirrored in our eyes, before lifting my bottle to my lips—every drop tasted like freedom amid this nightmare, a fleeting glimpse of hope in a world that sought to strip it away from us.

I watched in horror as the clock ticked past two hours, each second stretching out into an eternity, a cruel reminder of our desperate situation. Nothing could have prepared me for what happened next.

Harry, once buoyant and full of energy, bobbed beneath the surface, his body growing slack as exhaustion claimed him like a thief in the night. Panic surged through me, igniting my insides like wildfire, threatening to consume me whole.

"Harry!" I shouted, my voice cracking against the oppressive silence that had settled over the courtyard like a heavy fog. I couldn't bear it any longer, the helplessness clawing at my throat.

Without a moment's hesitation, Meg shot forward, her instincts kicking in as she reached for him. "I've got you!" she called out, her arms outstretched, determination blazing in her eyes like a beacon in the dark.

But before she could grasp Harry's hand, a guard stepped forward, brandishing a gun with a menacing grin etched across his face that sent a chill down my spine. The cold metal glinted ominously under the harsh sun, a stark reminder of our fragility.

"Back off!" he barked, leveling the weapon at Meg with a confidence that made my stomach twist in knots. The air turned electric with tension, and my heart raced, pounding in my ears louder than any command given that day, drowning out reason and hope alike.

"No!" I screamed again, the word bursting from my lips in a desperate plea, but my voice fell on deaf ears, swallowed by the suffocating atmosphere.

Mrs. Smith's voice cut through the chaos with chilling clarity, each word dripping with authority. "Anyone who attempts to help another will face *severe* consequences," she announced with an unsettling calmness that sent shivers racing down my spine. "This is your final warning."

My breath caught in my throat as Meg froze mid- reach, her eyes wide with fear and disbelief, mirroring the horror that clutched at my heart. The guard stood rigidly at her side, gun still aimed threateningly in her direction, the threat of violence hanging heavy in the air.

Desiree clutched my arm tightly, her knuckles white as she shared in my horror, a silent understanding passing between us. I could feel her tremble beside me, a reflection of my own dread mirrored back, our shared fear binding us in this moment of uncertainty.

I looked back at Harry; his head bobbed lower beneath the water now, and I felt desperation clawing at my insides, wild and feral, fighting to break free from the cage of helplessness. Each moment felt heavier than the last as time stretched painfully onward, mocking us with its relentless march.

"Don't give up!" I shouted to him, hoping somehow my words would penetrate through the haze of darkness creeping around him, reaching him like a lifeline thrown into turbulent waters.

But all I could do was watch as fear threatened to consume us all—fear of losing each other to this sick game they forced us into, a twisted reality where compassion was met with brutality.

The guards shifted uneasily; one glanced nervously at Mrs. Smith for direction while keeping their weapons raised high and ready to fire at any hint of rebellion among us, the slightest movement could trigger their wrath.

The atmosphere felt thick with unspoken tension— the kind that stifled breath and made it impossible to think clearly amidst this nightmare unfolding right before our eyes, each second a reminder of our vulnerability, our humanity under siege.

I watched in horror as Harry bobbed further under the water, and then he didn't come back up. My heart stopped, a sharp pain radiating through my chest.

"Harry!" My voice broke as I screamed his name, desperation clawing at my throat. Panic surged through me, overwhelming my senses. How could this be happening? The rules of this cruel game stripped us of our humanity, turning friends into mere numbers.

Meg lunged forward again, but the guard yelled, gun raised with a cruel smirk that sent chills down my spine. "You want to join him?" he taunted, the threat hanging in the air like a dark cloud.

"No! Someone save him!" I shouted, pushing against Desiree's grip on my arm. I felt the adrenaline coursing through me, fueling my resolve to save Harry despite the danger that loomed over us.

The water rippled as panic washed over the group like an infectious wave. I saw Quinn cover her mouth with trembling hands, tears brimming in her eyes as she processed what was happening. "He can't—he can't drown!" she whimpered, looking from me to Meg and back again.

But Harry was slipping away; I could see it now—his body going limp beneath the surface as if surrendering to the depths. Every second felt like an eternity stretched taut with fear and helplessness.

Another guard barked orders at us to step back while Mrs. Smith observed with her usual detached interest —a predator relishing its prey's suffering.

"Harry!" The word escaped my lips again, raw and ragged as it echoed across the courtyard. "Please!"

But there was only silence where laughter and camaraderie had once thrived among us; now it was replaced by dread and despair. As time stretched painfully onward, I felt an aching weight settle over me—a burden of sorrow and loss for a friend who might not come back.

The world around me blurred into a haze of confusion as everything seemed to collapse under the weight of this moment—the guard's gun aimed at Meg as she still tread water and Harry's absence consuming me whole.

A portion of me cried out to take action—to leap in after him—but another part remained paralyzed by terror, and I understood he was already lost.

Chapter 20

Connor

I paced the room, the phone pressed to my ear, and the seconds seemed to stretch into hours. It had been three agonizingly long hours since the announcement, and still, I had yet to hear anything concrete about Jessica's fate. The tension coiled tightly in my gut, a relentless reminder of my anxiety as I waited for Camilla to pick up.

"Sir," her voice buzzed through the receiver, shattering the oppressive quiet, yet it was evident she was attempting to conceal my identity.

"Camilla, what's happening? Are they alright?" My heart raced, pounding against my ribs as I struggled to keep my tone steady despite the unease gnawing at me.

"I'm outside the center now," she replied, a tremor of anxiety creeping into her words, betraying her calm facade. "A few other Center Hunters are here with me. We're trying to get updates, but it's chaos inside. I heard some yelling earlier, but nothing that gives us clarity."

I clenched my fists, frustration bubbling up like a volcano ready to erupt. "Yelling? What kind of yelling?"

"Just voices raised—nothing specific." She sighed heavily, the sound heavy with concern. "They changed guards during the commotion. I managed to ask one of them about Jessica's condition, but I haven't seen him since."

Rubbing my temples, I fought off a wave of panic that threatened to consume me. "What if they—"

"Stop," she interrupted sharply, her voice like a cold splash of water. "We can't jump to conclusions. Focus on what we know."

"And what is that?" My voice turned brittle, cracking under the weight of my fears.

She hesitated for a moment, and I could almost feel her weighing each word carefully before speaking again. "The guards seemed… different after the announcement. They were more on edge than usual."

"What does that mean for Jessica?" The knot in my stomach twisted tighter, squeezing the breath from my lungs.

"I don't know yet," she admitted reluctantly, her tone laced with uncertainty. "But I'll keep trying to gather intel from here."

The silence hung heavy between us, a suffocating presence, before she continued, "Sir… just remember that you need to stay calm too."

I leaned against the wall, feeling the rough texture beneath my palm grounding me as much as it could in this moment of uncertainty. "You think they'd really hurt her? Even knowing that she's been claimed?"

"We've seen them act with cruelty before," she said softly, her words a chilling reminder of the world we lived in.

"Damn it!" I snapped, frustration spilling over into anger, the helplessness of it all clawing at my insides.

"Listen," Camilla said firmly, her tone sharpening like steel, cutting through my turmoil. "We're not giving up on her. I am not leaving until I have answers."

Taking a deep breath, I tried to channel that determination into something productive—a plan, a distraction—but all I felt was this insatiable urge to protect her from whatever storm was brewing within those walls. The weight of my responsibility pressed down on me, and I knew I had to be strong, not just for myself, but for Jessica, for all of us.

I leaned closer to the phone, my breath hitching as Camilla switched it to speaker mode. The crisp click echoed in the silence, amplifying the tension that hung in the air, and my heart raced in response. I could hear her shuffling, the sound of her adjusting the angle as she strained to catch every word without drawing attention to our covert operation.

"Alright, let's see what they're saying," she murmured, her voice barely above a whisper, laced with an urgency that mirrored my own.

I inhaled sharply upon hearing the Center Liaison's voice. Her refined articulation stood in stark contrast to the turmoil churning in my thoughts. Each syllable she uttered felt like a carefully crafted façade; she spoke with an overly cheerful tone—too bright and artificial—as though she were greeting attendees at a lavish event instead of managing a place that thrived on dread and despair.

"Welcome, Center Hunters!" Mrs. Smith trilled, her tone dripping with insincerity, masking any tension lurking beneath the surface. "We've prepared an update for you in our conference room."

"What a performance," I muttered under my breath, disgust pooling in my stomach like a thick sludge. It was infuriating to witness such a display of false cheerfulness when the stakes were so incredibly high.

Camilla quieted me softly over the phone, a gentle prompt that I needed to silence my frustration and pay attention to Mrs. Smith's forthcoming remarks. I could feel the weight of this moment pressing down on me, urging me to stay focused.

"Please follow me; we have much to discuss regarding the recent developments." Her voice cut through the static as I heard the group of Center Hunters shuffling behind her like sheep following a shepherd into unknown territory, oblivious to the danger that loomed ahead.

"What's going on?" I asked myself absently, frustration creeping back into my voice, tightening my throat. The uncertainty felt like a vise, squeezing my chest as the implications of her words sank in.

My mind raced with possibilities: what if they were deciding Jessica's fate? Would they punish her for something she hadn't even done? The thought sent a jolt of panic coursing through me, gnawing at my insides like a wolf ready to strike. All I could do was wait for answers as anxiety clawed at me, relentless and unforgiving.

I rested against the frigid wall of my office, feeling the chill seep into my bones as I eavesdropped on Camilla's conversation. She must have secured a prime spot nearby since I could clearly hear Mrs. Smith, her voice cutting through the air with an unsettling clarity.

"Thank you for gathering on such short notice," she began, her tone smooth yet chillingly devoid of empathy, like ice sliding down a mountainside. "We have an urgent matter to address regarding the recent behavior of several center participants."

A ripple of anxiety coursed through me, igniting a primal instinct to protect those I cared about. My fingers clenched into fists at my sides, straining against the tension mounting in the air, each heartbeat echoing in my ears like a war drum.

"Several participants engaged in acts that were deemed treasonous," she stated flatly, as if discussing last week's weather rather than lives hanging in the balance. "I understand this may affect some of your assignments currently set up. No one will blame you if your participant is no longer of interest due to their behavior." The way she said it— like it was a mere inconvenience—made my stomach churn and my mind race with the implications.

"In order to cancel a request for a participant who has acted against their country," Mrs. Smith explained, "the process is quite simple." She paused, letting her words settle like dust before revealing the next bombshell, each second stretching into an eternity.

"The consequences today to bring order to the group were drastic," she said, her tone chillingly nonchalant. "One participant did not survive."

My heart dropped like a stone, disbelief crashing over me in waves; I could hardly wrap my mind around what she had just said. "Didn't survive?" I whispered under my breath, the outrage bubbling up like molten lava, barely contained.

Mrs. Smith continued without missing a beat, brushing aside any semblance of humanity with her next words. "While this is tragic for some, we consider it a blessing—he had not been claimed and fulfilled his duty to his country by teaching others never to rebel again."

The line fell silent, suffocating beneath the weight of her callousness. My blood boiled as anger surged through me like fire igniting dry wood, crackling with intensity. How could she dismiss a life so casually? How could anyone view death as an effective lesson? The thought twisted in my gut, fueling my determination to stand against this monstrous system, to fight for those who couldn't fight for themselves. I wouldn't let her cruelty go unchallenged.

I clenched my jaw as Mrs. Smith's voice sliced through the tension, her words dripping with a chilling indifference. "As I mentioned, four participants are ready for their assignments due to their elimination. The other three will be packed up to go to their holding facility for trials."

The words struck me like a physical blow, and I felt the air grow thick around me. She didn't just talk about lives; she spoke of futures, of hopes dashed against the jagged rocks of this twisted system. Each participant was a person, not just a number or an asset to be discarded.

My fingers curled into fists at my sides, fighting against the urge to storm in there and confront her about the life she so carelessly disregarded. Who was she to dictate someone's fate with such arrogance?

"You will each have access to your assigned participants during this transition." She paused, glancing around the room as if gauging our reactions before adding, "But know that they will be closely monitored."

I gulped, suppressing my fury and unease as I concentrated on the gravity of her statements. Jessica required my support now more than ever. Just imagining her grappling with the nightmare she had endured set my blood on fire. The idea of anyone subjecting her to a trial made that fire explode. I grabbed my phone, messaging Jonathan that he and Mia had to hit the road without delay.

"Every Center Hunter plays a part in making sure their participant adjusts properly," Mrs. Smith went on. "Every participant facing trial has at least two individuals eager to meet them." The way she emphasized the word meeting sent a chill down my back. And the thought that if she won, someone else had asked to trial Jessica was unacceptable; I wouldn't allow that to occur.

The line hummed with a tense energy; everyone was grappling with what had just been revealed. Four participants were off to their assignments while three would face an even darker path—a chilling thought that hung heavily in the air.

I felt determination swell within me like a tidal wave, crashing against the despair threatening to pull me under. Jessica wouldn't be just another casualty; I refused to let that happen.

"Get your participants ready," Mrs. Smith commanded abruptly, breaking the spell of silence that had fallen over us. "The ones who are going to trial have a few hours."

As murmurs filled the room and everyone shifted into action, my heart raced at the thought of finding Jessica again amidst this chaos. Time was running out; I needed to ensure she wouldn't be lost in this ruthless game any longer than necessary.

I heard the echo of Camilla's heels clacking against the polished floor as she exited the center, her voice barely a whisper in the tense atmosphere. "Did you catch all that?"

"Yes, I'm dispatching staff to the holding facility. She requires support before her next center," I replied, my mind racing with the implications of her words.

"No, I don't think you grasp the situation. She is among the final three. She's on her way to trial. I'll see what I can do to eliminate that other interest," Camilla said, her tone sharp and commanding, laced with urgency.

I clenched my jaw, feeling the weight of the moment settle heavily on my shoulders. "Jonathan, my assistant, is on his way. He'll take my place when meeting her. He's to stay in her apartment for as long as he can; he won't leave her alone until she's coming to our wedding." The words tasted bitter on my tongue, but I knew I had to do whatever it took to protect Jessica. She couldn't slip away from me—not now, not ever.

After hanging up with Camilla, I glanced at my phone and noted with a mix of relief and urgency that Jonathan and Mia were as reliable as ever; they were already en route to the city, their commitment unwavering. I shot Jonathan a quick text, hoping to convey the gravity of the situation without overwhelming him.

Connor: Head to the holding facility. You're stepping in for me during the trials; stay with her the whole time. I'm counting on you to keep her safe, but you are NOT to touch her. His response came almost instantly, a testament to his efficiency and loyalty.

Jonathan: Understood, Boss! My love is solely for Carolynn, but I'll protect your girl. Why is Mia with me if she can't go inside?

I could almost picture his confident smirk as he typed, and it provided me with a moment of comfort amidst the chaos.

Connor: She's her best friend. You have two hours to gather everything you can to show her that we can be trusted.

I hit send and leaned back, a knot of anxiety twisting in my stomach. I had to trust Jonathan and Mia, but every second felt like an eternity, and the stakes were impossibly high. Jessica's future depended on it.

Mia

The car hummed along the road, a constant, almost soothing sound that belied the tension thick in the air between us. I glanced sideways at Jonathan, who gripped the steering wheel with a focus that made my stomach churn with unease. His jaw was set tight, and the way he concentrated on the road ahead was unnerving, as if he were trying to steer us away from a fate we both dreaded.

"Look, Mia," he said, his voice steady but low, cutting through the silence like a knife. "These trials are...

complicated. They let potential husbands test out their future wives, see if they are what they *want* before making any commitments."

I nodded slowly, digesting his words as they sunk deep into my mind. The thought of Jessica being violated and treated like some sort of prize, something to be evaluated and discarded at will, unsettled me to my core. It felt wrong on so many levels, and I could feel the anger bubbling just beneath the surface. "It's disgusting," I muttered, my voice barely above a whisper, but the rage simmering within me was palpable.

"They want to make sure she's *compatible* and good enough," Jonathan continued, keeping his eyes riveted on the road, but I could see the tension in his shoulders. "I've been told to stay in her suite and ensure no one else gets near her. And I need to convince her he's a good guy without revealing too much."

"Yeah? How do you plan to do that?" I shot back, my heart racing at the idea of him needing to sugarcoat a situation that was anything but sweet. The thought of spinning this into something positive made my insides twist, but I knew it had to be done for Jessica's sake. "You can't just tell her he's nice. She'll want to know the truth."

Jonathan sighed, rubbing the back of his neck as if trying to ease the weight of his responsibilities. "That's where you come in. You know Jess better than anyone."

"Right." I leaned back in my seat, my mind racing through ideas, trying to think of anything that might make this easier for her. "You have to emphasize that it's a small household. Tell her Mr. Dandin is kind and gives her space—freedom even—to be herself."

He glanced over at me, eyebrows raised in surprise. "Freedom?"

"Exactly! Make it sound like she'll have control over her life there." My thoughts tumbled out as I spoke, fueled by a fierce protectiveness for my friend. "And focus on how she'll be safe and looked after—like she's stepping into a new chapter instead of being trapped again. She needs to believe that this is a chance for her to thrive, not just survive."

Jonathan nodded slowly, clearly considering my words. "That makes sense," he murmured, but I could see the doubt still lurking in his eyes. "What if she doesn't believe me?"

"If you can get her to see the positives without scaring her off, she might trust you," I added quickly, trying to mask my own unease about the situation. "You just have to stay focused on her needs, Jonathan. We can't let her feel like she's being sold off. She deserves to feel valued."

He took a deep breath as we approached the holding center's entrance, the building looming ahead like a dark cloud overhead, casting a shadow over my racing thoughts. "Thanks for your help," he said quietly, glancing at me before returning his gaze to the road, where the asphalt seemed to stretch endlessly ahead.

"Just keep Jess safe," I replied firmly, my voice steady despite the whirlwind of emotions swirling within me. "And remember, if you see anything off, you need to act fast. We can't let her get caught up in something that's going to break her spirit."

Jonathan nodded, his expression serious. "I will. I promise."

As we pulled into a parking space, the weight of our mission pressed down on us both. "I can't believe we're actually doing this," I said, trying to shake off the anxiety that had settled in my chest. "It feels like we're walking into a trap."

"Maybe," he replied, his tone thoughtful. "But we have to try. For her."

The chill in the air was a stark reminder of the uncertainty that lay ahead and the urgency of our task. I took a deep breath, steeling myself for what was to come. "Let's just hope we're not too late," I murmured, my determination hardening as we stepped out into the cool air.

As we stepped out of the car, the atmosphere around the holding facility felt heavy with uncertainty. The building loomed over us like a giant sentinel, and I couldn't shake the chill creeping up my spine. Jonathan led the way, his focus unwavering as he approached the entrance.

At the door, a tall guy with sandy hair and a warm smile leaned against the wall, arms crossed. He straightened when he spotted Jonathan. "Hey, Jonathan," he called out, pushing off the wall and stepping forward.

"Brad," Jonathan replied with a nod, relief washing over his face. "Glad to see you."

"Likewise." Brad's eyes flicked to me before returning to Jonathan. "So what brings you here?"

"I'm on Mr. Dandin's orders," Jonathan said, lowering his voice slightly. "I'm here for Jessica's trial. I'll be waiting in her suite." He gestured toward me. "This is Mia—she's another member of the staff. We need to keep her safe while I'm in there with Jessica."

Brad studied me for a moment before nodding slowly. "Alright then, let's get you settled." He turned on his heel and led us through the entrance, where a sterile corridor stretched ahead.

I followed closely behind them, my heart racing as we moved deeper into the facility. Brad guided us past rooms with doors marked by numbers instead of names—each one a potential prison or sanctuary for whoever resided inside.

"Jessica is lucky to have you two," Brad said over his shoulder as we walked.

Jonathan shrugged off the compliment but didn't deny it either. "We're just doing what we can."

Eventually, Brad stopped at a door marked "Staff Lounge" and pushed it open. Inside was a small room furnished with mismatched chairs and a table that had seen better days. The walls were bare except for one framed picture—a faded image of what looked like some sort of nature scene.

"Wait here," Brad instructed us as he stepped inside to assess things further.

I glanced at Jonathan, feeling a mix of anxiety and

determination bubbling within me. "Do you really think we can keep Jessica safe?" I asked quietly.

He nodded, though I noticed a flicker of doubt in his eyes. "We have to believe that," he replied firmly.

Brad returned, leaning against the doorframe with an easy confidence that eased some of my tension. "You'll be fine in here until everything gets sorted out," he assured me before turning back to Jonathan. "You ready?"

Jonathan took a deep breath, his resolve solidifying as he prepared to face whatever lay ahead for Jessica in that suite—his loyalty unshakeable despite the stakes rising higher than ever before.

Chapter 21

Jessica

I sat on the edge of my bed, my heart pounding as shock settled in like a heavy blanket, wrapping around me, squeezing out all rational thought. The silence in the room felt suffocating, thick and oppressive, making it hard to breathe. My hands trembled uncontrollably, and I could hear muffled sobs around me—Desiree's quiet cries mingling with my own anguish, forming a haunting symphony of despair. Harry's face lingered in my mind, his desperate struggle against the water flashing before my eyes like a terrible nightmare I couldn't escape.

The guards moved through the center like ominous shadows, their expressions cold and unyielding, devoid of any empathy or understanding. They pointed at Annie and Aaron, their fingers jabbing in our direction with ruthless precision, instructing them to stand. The sight of my friends being singled out sent a jolt of panic through me, a visceral response that twisted my insides.

"Wait! No!" I choked out, my voice barely rising above the chaos swirling in my mind, thin and fragile like glass. Every heartbeat felt like a desperate plea, a last attempt to hold onto them, to keep them close in this horrifying reality.

Annie shot me a pained look, her eyes wide with fear, as they were escorted away, those moments stretching into eternity. I could see her brother's hand slipping from hers, an agonizing moment of separation that felt like a physical blow, a fracture in our world just before they vanished through the heavy door, leaving a suffocating silence in their wake.

Jake followed next, his tall frame towering over the guard, yet somehow he remained compliant, his shoulders slumped under the weight of the situation. I reached for him, my fingers stretching out in a desperate bid for connection, hoping he could feel my fear and frustration, that he could somehow reassure me that everything would be alright.

"Don't go!" Meg called out, her voice cracking as panic clawed at her throat, the sound raw and desperate, mirroring the turmoil churning inside me like a storm.

Meg's cries echoed through the room, a haunting reminder of our shared dread, as Jake turned to offer one last reassuring smile before he disappeared into the hall. "I'll be okay!" he shouted back, but even as he said it, the words felt hollow, lacking the conviction we all desperately needed. The reality of our separation hit me hard, leaving a gaping void where our camaraderie once stood, a chasm of uncertainty and fear.

As if we were all trapped in a twisted game of fate, Meg was next. The guard, unyielding in his duty, began to lead her away despite her desperate pleas for just one last moment with us. "Please! Let me say goodbye!" Her voice fractured mid-sentence, a heartbreaking sound that echoed down the cold, sterile corridor until it faded into an unbearable silence. I could almost feel the weight of her fear pressing against me, a tangible reminder of what we were losing. I wanted to reach out, to hold her back, but the reality of our situation stifled my movements, leaving me frozen in place, helpless and aching for her to stay just a little longer.

Then Mrs. Smith appeared, her heels clicking against the floor like a metronome marking our doom, each step amplifying the dread coiling in my stomach. She strode toward us with an air of authority, her expression as unyielding as the polished tiles beneath her feet. As her steely gaze swept over Desiree, Paige, and me, I felt the weight of her look settle on my shoulders, a chilling reminder of the fate that awaited us. It was as if I were standing before an executioner, stripped of hope and left vulnerable in a world that had turned its back on us.

"You three will be heading to holding facilities for your trials," she announced flatly, her voice devoid of any warmth or empathy, just a stark declaration of our grim reality. The words hung in the air, heavy and suffocating, as if sealing our fates in a way we couldn't escape, a grim verdict that echoed in my ears.

My stomach sank at the mention of those words— trials? I rifled through my memory, recalling the man in the elevator with blood on his knuckles. I couldn't imagine it happening to me, especially as they led Desiree away first, leaving Paige and me quaking on our beds, our minds racing with dread.

"Jessica," Mrs. Smith gestured for me to follow her, her voice sharp and commanding. My legs felt like lead as I rose to comply, the weight of dread settling heavily on my chest, each step feeling like a march toward the unknown.

I stepped outside into the biting cold air, where a sleek black car idled ominously by the curb, its presence a stark reminder of the grim reality that awaited me, looming like a dark cloud. Camilla waited inside, her expression unreadable and distant as I climbed in beside her, the door shutting with a finality that made my heart race, a door closing on the last remnants of hope.

Once we pulled away from the center's imposing walls and headed into the oppressive darkness, I felt the dam inside me break. I couldn't hold it together any longer. "Camilla," I sobbed between gasps for breath, my voice trembling with anguish, each word breaking free like a desperate wail. "Harry… he… they let him die… he's gone!"

Her eyes softened for a brief moment, a flicker of understanding breaking through the hardened facade, but just as quickly, she steeled herself once more against my grief, as if my pain was an inconvenience she couldn't bear to face. As we drove further away from the worst day of my life—

everything that had just shattered like glass around me—I poured out my heart, recounting every moment of horror, every image that splashed across my memory like ink on paper, staining my thoughts with despair and leaving me feeling utterly alone in a world that felt increasingly dark and unforgiving.

∞∞∞∞∞

As the car rolled to a stop outside the Holding Facility, my heart raced with a tumultuous mix of dread and uncertainty. The darkened building loomed before me, its jagged edges and oppressive façade more intimidating than I remembered from my last visit. I could feel the weight of my fears pressing against my chest, each breath a reminder of what was at stake. Camilla turned to me, her expression softening for just a fleeting moment, as if she were trying to share a piece of her strength. But almost instantly, she masked it with the professionalism I had come to expect from her, reverting to the stoic demeanor that had become a shield between us.

"Jessica," she said, her voice steady yet laced with an urgency that made me sit up straighter in my seat. "You need to be confident. Remember who you are. You're strong. Don't let them break you." Her words echoed in my mind, reverberating like a mantra as I opened the door and stepped out into the biting cold air. I took a deep breath, letting the crispness wash over me, steeling myself against the chill that threatened to seep into my very bones. Each step I took toward the entrance felt heavier than the last, as if the weight of my fears clung to me like an unwanted shadow. But I reminded myself: I had to be strong, for myself and for those who believed in me, for Brad and my friends who were counting on me.

"Good luck," Camilla called after me, her voice fading into the cold air, but I didn't turn back. I couldn't afford to show weakness, not now—not when everything I cared about hung in the balance. I pressed forward, each step a battle against the uncertainty swirling in my mind, the looming structure a constant reminder of the challenges ahead.

Brad met me at the entrance, his familiar presence instantly reassuring as he ushered me inside with quick, purposeful steps. "Hurry," he urged, his voice low and urgent, cutting through the tension that enveloped me like a heavy fog. "I've heard it's been a tough day, but you need to be strong and move quickly. We don't have much time." I could hear the concern in his tone, a reminder that this wasn't just about me anymore; others were counting on me too, and the gravity of that responsibility weighed heavily on my heart.

I nodded, my heart pounding a frantic rhythm in my chest as he led me toward a private elevator tucked away from prying eyes, a hidden sanctuary amidst the chaos. The metallic doors slid shut behind us, sealing away the outside world, and I felt a fleeting sense of relief wash over me. Once inside, Brad leaned closer, his face serious and intent as he lowered his voice even further. "The man is already in your suite," he whispered urgently, his eyes darting toward the elevator doors, as if expecting someone to come bursting through at any moment. "It's someone I know and trust completely."

"What do you mean?" Panic surged through me, a wave of dread crashing over the fragile resolve I had worked so hard to maintain. I felt my breath quicken, my mind racing with the possibilities and implications of his words. Who was waiting for me? And could I truly trust them? Each question felt like a weight, adding to the suffocating pressure in my chest.

"There's a second man who isn't safe," he continued swiftly, his tone serious and laced with urgency. "He's trying to get you for trial." My stomach churned at his words—trials were never good news. They were the kind of news that could unravel everything, shattering the fragile threads of safety I clung to, and the thought sent a shiver down my spine.

"Listen closely," he said, gripping my shoulder firmly, his fingers digging in as if trying to ground me in this storm of confusion and fear. I could feel the warmth of his hand, a stark contrast to the chill creeping up my spine, a chilling reminder of the uncertainty that loomed over me. "No matter how long it takes or what happens, you have to let the man currently in your suite stay there until I come back and tell you it's safe." His gaze bore into mine, an intense mixture of concern and determination that made my heart race, sending a jolt of adrenaline coursing through my veins. I swallowed hard, the weight of his words settling like a stone in my stomach. What choice did I really have? Trusting him felt like a gamble, but the alternative was too terrifying to consider, a future I couldn't bear to imagine.

Before I could muster a response, Brad ushered me out of the elevator, his movements brisk and decisive, as if propelling me through the chaos that threatened to consume me. We moved quickly toward my familiar suite, each step echoing my growing anxiety, the passageway seeming to stretch infinitely before me. The door creaked open with an all-too-familiar sound that sent shivers down my spine, a reminder of everything that lay beyond it—a space that felt both like sanctuary and a potential trap, a delicate balance of hope and fear.

"Go inside," he urged softly but firmly, his voice a steady anchor in the storm of my emotions.

I stepped over the threshold into the room filled with mixed memories of warmth and despair, the scent of home and the lingering shadows of past heartaches intertwining in the air like ghosts of my former self.

My heart raced as I froze at the sight of a mystery man standing at my kitchen counter. He looked up from whatever he was doing and smiled gently—a stranger yet somehow comforting amid chaos—and my pulse quickened again in both fear and uncertainty about what lay ahead. What was he expecting from me? I could feel the weight of questions pressing against my chest, each one a knot of anxiety tightening inside me, threatening to unravel the fragile composure I had fought so hard to maintain.

I stepped inside, my heart pounding in my chest like a drum as I took in the sight of the man at the counter. He turned to face me, and a warm smile broke across his face, radiating an unexpected comfort that sent a flicker of curiosity through me, mingling with the fear that clung to my insides like a second skin.

"Hey there," he said, his voice calm and reassuring, cutting through the tension that had settled in the air. "I'm Jonathan." He extended a hand toward me, open and inviting, but I hesitated, my instincts screaming to hold back. I wasn't ready to trust anyone —not yet. The world had taught me caution, and each moment felt like a delicate balance between hope and apprehension.

"I'm here on behalf of my boss," he continued, lowering his hand when I didn't respond. His gesture felt like an olive branch, but I remained rooted in my trepidation. "I promise you, I mean no harm. I won't hurt you or even touch you." His sincerity washed over me like a gentle wave, easing some of the tension that had gripped me since Brad had left. Yet, even as his words wrapped around me like a comforting blanket, doubts still lingered in my mind, whispering caution with every heartbeat.

"Why would your boss be interested in me?" I asked, crossing my arms defensively, creating a barrier that seemed to pulse with my uncertainty. The question hung between us like an invisible wall, thick with my apprehension. My heart raced, the rhythm quickening in my chest; why was this stranger here? What did he want from me? Each moment felt like a fragile thread, threatening to snap under the weight of my worries.

Jonathan shifted his weight slightly, a flicker of concern passing over his face, as if he were wrestling with the weight of the words he was about to share. "There's a long history behind it," he said carefully, his voice steady yet tinged with unease. "Only my boss can explain it fully. But believe me when I say he has watched you through all your centers." He paused for a moment, gauging my reaction with those keen eyes of his, searching for signs of understanding, or perhaps disbelief, before continuing. "He's tried his hardest to help you when he could."

I frowned at him, my brow furrowing as I struggled to piece together the fragmented puzzle of his words. Help? The notion felt foreign, almost surreal. All those times I had felt so utterly alone and abandoned —lost in the cold, sterile walls of the centers— someone had been watching? The idea sent a shiver down my spine, making me feel both vulnerable and strangely comforted. It was a dichotomy that left me reeling; the thought that someone cared enough to observe, even from a distance, was a balm to my aching spirit, yet it also stirred a whirlwind of questions. Why hadn't I known? What could he possibly want from me?

"He wants to protect you," Jonathan added softly, his eyes earnest and unwavering, offering a glimmer of hope that I desperately needed. "It's a small household he manages; very secluded and safe. You wouldn't have to worry about the chaos of the centers anymore. No more being a second-class citizen. No more worrying about the future of your life." His words wrapped around me like a warm blanket, promising safety and solace in a world that had always felt so harsh and unforgiving.

"And how do I know you're telling the truth?" I asked, my voice wavering slightly as doubt crept back in, like an unwelcome shadow lurking just out of sight. The uncertainty gnawed at me; I had been burned before by false promises and whispered lies. How could I trust that this time would be different?

"You'll just have to trust me," he replied with a slight shrug, his expression steady but kind, as though he could sense the turmoil swirling inside me.

I bit my lip, caught in a tempest of emotions. Part of me desperately wanted to believe him, to cling to the hope that perhaps this time would be different. But another part, shadowed by past betrayals, screamed at me to be cautious. The events of the day crashed over me like waves in a storm—first the chaos of the revolt, the cutthroat competition that had stripped away my sense of safety, and then the gut-wrenching moment of being torn from my new friends who had become my lifeline in a world that felt increasingly hostile. Now, here I was, standing before a stranger who was asking me to take a leap of faith. The weight of uncertainty pressed down on me, and I felt myself shut down, retreating into a protective shell that had become all too familiar.

Chapter 22

Jessica

Three days passed in a haze of unexpected companionship that both surprised and soothed me. Jonathan and I settled into a rhythm that felt oddly comforting, almost like a warm blanket in the midst of the swirling chaos that enveloped my life. By the second day, the tension that had filled the air between us had dissipated like morning mist under the gentle caress of the sun, leaving behind an easy friendship that I hadn't anticipated. I found myself laughing more, sharing thoughts I had kept tucked away, and feeling a sense of normalcy that had been absent for so long. It was strange how quickly we had grown to rely on one another, but in that moment, it felt right.

"Are you sure you want to try this?" he asked, a brotherly glint dancing in his eyes as we gathered our ingredients to make pizza. I couldn't help but smile at his enthusiasm, the way his energy filled the room with an almost palpable excitement. The kitchen, stark and simple, yearned for life and love, its sterile surfaces and muted colors contrasting sharply with the warmth of our budding friendship. I could almost imagine how the space would transform as we mixed flour and water, laughter echoing off the walls, and the aroma of freshly baked dough filling the air.

"Absolutely," I replied, a smile breaking across my face, brightening the mood even further. The corners of my lips lifted involuntarily, the sheer joy of the moment washing over me like a warm wave. "What's life without a little cheese?" The words rolled off my tongue with a carefree spirit, the kind I had almost forgotten I possessed, buried beneath the weight of my worries and the expectations that often felt like chains. In that instant, I felt lighter, as if the mere thought of pizza could momentarily free me from the confines of my reality.

As we combined flour and water, our laughter reverberated through the room, blending with the aromas of the aged wood and spices. The dough transformed into our masterpiece; Jonathan patiently guided me on how to stretch it perfectly without ripping, his skilled hands directing mine. He recounted how the cook had taught him shortly before his visit, and it was clear from the way he spoke of her that he was smitten. I stumbled a bit, my fingers sliding in the sticky mixture, but I chuckled, the sound rising like the yeast we had incorporated. Flour adorned my cheeks like a light dusting of powdered sugar, leaving a subtle trace of joy that seemed to emanate from within. The moment felt almost dreamlike—here I was, separated from everything familiar, yet I discovered a surprising delight in creating pizza with someone who had once intimidated me, his laughter now a soothing tune that dispelled my worries.

We set the pizzas on trays and slid them into the oven, the warm aroma of rising dough mingling with the anticipation of our game. With a sense of camaraderie, we plopped down at the table, the chessboard between us like a battlefield waiting for our strategies to unfold. Jonathan's concentration was intense, his brow furrowing as he plotted his moves, while I did my best to keep pace with his rapidly evolving strategy.

"You know," he said during one of my turns, breaking the comfortable silence, "the mansion has beautiful grounds but nothing has been decorated. My boss hasn't decorated a single room since he moved in."

I furrowed my brow at him, curiosity sparking within me. "Why not? If it's such a nice place, it seems like a waste…"

"Don't know," he shrugged, leaning back in his chair with an easy grin that made my heart flutter slightly at the feeling of having new friends. "There are only five of us on staff right now— my boss included—and all of us live in guest rooms despite having actual staff quarters that have been left empty."

"That sounds abnormal," I remarked, my mind racing as I tried to envision what life must be like in that grand yet neglected space, where echoes of elegance lingered amid the dust and shadows, whispering stories of a time when the mansion was alive with activity and beauty. I could almost picture the lavish gatherings that must have taken place there, laughter and music filling the air, now replaced by an unsettling quiet.

"It is," he admitted, a hint of weariness creeping into his voice as he leaned forward, his expression reflecting a deeper understanding of the situation. "But there's room to build more if needed. He just hasn't needed to." His words hung in the air, heavy with unspoken possibilities, making me wonder what transformations could happen if someone decided to breathe new life into that forgotten place.

I pondered this revelation as our pizzas baked, the timer ticking down like a heartbeat—a small flicker of hope igniting within me. Perhaps there was more than just survival waiting for me outside these walls; maybe there could be rebuilding too, a chance to create something beautiful from the remnants of what once was.

After finishing our game—my defeat met with light-hearted teasing that felt like warm sunlight breaking through the clouds—we settled on the couch to watch another questionable movie. The laughter continued to bubble between us like freshly popped popcorn, an effervescent reminder that, even amidst uncertainty, moments of joy could still be found, making me forget about everything else—even if only for just a little while.

I jumped at the sound of the key turning in the lock, my heart racing like a wild drum in my chest. The familiar anxiety surged through me, a sensation I had grown all too accustomed to. Jonathan shot to his feet, urgency replacing our light-hearted banter in an instant, the playful atmosphere vanishing as quickly as it had come.

"Lock yourself in the bedroom," he commanded, his voice low but firm, a seriousness that sent a shiver down my spine. "Stay there until I say it's safe." I could hear the underlying tension in his words, the weight of the situation pressing down on us, and I nodded, my mind racing with worry as I made my way toward the bedroom, each step filled with dread about what could be waiting for us on the other side of that door.

Before I could protest, he ushered me toward the door. I felt a surge of panic but obeyed, slipping into the bedroom and closing the door behind me. The click of the lock echoed in my ears as I leaned against it, my pulse pounding like a drum.

Moments later, I heard another door swing open, and the familiar cadence of Jonathan's voice collided with a new one—Brad's, steady yet filled with urgency.

"Is Mia okay?" Jonathan asked, his tone urgent, tinged with an underlying current of concern that made my heart race.

"She's back at the estate," Brad replied quickly, his words tumbling out with a sense of relief. "I drove her home myself. She's safe." The reassurance in his voice was a balm, but it did little to quell the unease that gnawed at me.

A rush of relief washed over me as I listened in on their discussion from behind the shut door. But how did they both know her? Was it my Mia? If Mia was alright, maybe everything else would work out too.

"Good," Jonathan said, his voice laced with a hint of relief, but then he paused, as if weighing his next words carefully. "I never thought we'd be stuck here for days."

From my hidden spot, I could hear Brad shuffling around in the main area, his movements punctuated by the sound of papers rustling as he filled Jonathan in on everything that had happened since I'd last seen them. Each noise stirred my curiosity and anxiety in equal measure.

"The potential trial was with Mr. Kline," Brad explained, his voice steady, yet I detected an undercurrent of tension that made my heart race once more. "It took him days to give up his claim on Jessica." His words hung in the air, heavy with implications, and I felt a cold shiver run down my spine at the mention of Mr. Kline. The thought of his relentless pursuit made my stomach churn, each second stretching as I hung on every detail, desperate for reassurance that I was still safe.

My stomach dropped at the mention of Kline's name; memories of his icy demeanor flooded my mind, sending chills down my spine that I couldn't shake off. The way he had looked at me, as if I were nothing more than a possession, made bile rise in my throat. But then came Brad's next words, which landed heavily in my chest like a blow I hadn't seen coming.

"Jessica has been officially claimed," he continued, his voice steady yet laden with an urgency that made my heart race. "We'll be heading to her wedding from here. I am coming with you; he's also somehow managed to get me reassigned to be part of his staff."

A rush of emotions crashed over me—fear mingled with disbelief and an odd flicker of hope that caught me off guard. A wedding? My wedding? The very thought was both thrilling and terrifying, and the fact that Brad was coming along provided a shred of comfort amidst the turmoil.

"It will be a small legal ceremony with just us—household staff," Brad clarified quickly, as if he could sense my confusion through the closed door. His tone was reassuring, but it did little to quell the storm brewing inside me. "But Mr. Dandin has promised you can plan her dream wedding with her family once she's back home."

Home? The idea felt surreal, almost unattainable, yet beneath the layers of dread and uncertainty, a part of me wanted to believe that this could be real—a chance to reclaim some semblance of normalcy amidst the chaos swirling around me. The thought of being surrounded by my family and friends, celebrating love instead of fear, was intoxicating.

Just then, Jonathan knocked lightly on the bedroom door, his voice breaking through the haze of my thoughts. "The coast is clear, Jess. You can come out now." His words were like a lifeline, offering me a moment of reprieve from the whirlwind of emotions that had taken hold of me.

I took a deep breath, steadying myself, and turned the knob, pushing the door open with a hesitant hand. The sight of Brad waiting for me on the other side, his expression serious yet reassuring, grounded me in the moment, anchoring my swirling thoughts.

"Hey," I said, forcing a smile that felt fragile as I stepped into the room, hoping it would mask the fear gnawing at my insides.

"Hey," he replied, a flicker of relief crossing his face as he took in my appearance, his eyes scanning for any signs of distress. "You okay?"

I nodded, though I could feel my heart racing beneath the surface, a frantic drumbeat echoing in my chest that betrayed the calm I tried to project.

"Should I be getting ready?" I asked, trying to keep my voice steady, even as I felt the tremor in my hands. The weight of the impending chaos pressed down on me, and I fought to maintain a façade of composure.

"Yeah," he said, urgency creeping into his tone, his brow furrowing slightly. "We need to move fast. Mr. Kline is furious, and we can't underestimate him." The gravity of his words hung in the air, reminding me of the perilous situation we faced, and I felt the adrenaline surge through my veins, heightening my senses as I prepared to step into the unknown.

The weight of his words pressed down on me like a heavy

blanket. "Traveling? Where are we going?"

"To the estate," he replied quickly, glancing at Jonathan as if silently communicating something important between them. "Once we're there, you can get ready for the ceremony."

"The ceremony?" The word felt foreign on my tongue. "What ceremony?" Panic bubbled up inside me like a shaken soda bottle.

Brad's eyes darted to Jonathan, and in that fleeting instant, a silent communication exchanged between them—one that only deepened my bewilderment. It felt as though they believed I might run away.

Jonathan cleared his throat awkwardly. "Just... a legal thing." His tone lacked conviction. "The legal marriage ceremony"

I narrowed my eyes at them both. "What about Mia? Who is she? The Mia you were talking about?" At that question, both their faces went pale, and I felt the air grow thick with tension.

"Mia?" Brad echoed, glancing sharply at Jonathan as if he'd just let slip something crucial. "Uh… she's just someone from your—"

"She's important to you," Jonathan interjected quickly, his eyes darting back and forth between us as if searching for a way out of this trap.

"But why was she in this conversation?" My curiosity burned hotter now than ever before, fueled by their hesitations.

Brad shifted uncomfortably on his feet while Jonathan opened his mouth to speak again but faltered under my gaze.

Something wasn't right; they weren't telling me everything.

"We should focus on getting you ready," Brad finally said firmly, clearly hoping to steer us away from this line of questioning.

But I wasn't ready to drop it yet; not when there were so many questions swirling around in my head like storm clouds waiting to burst open.

"Why was she in this conversation?" I pressed, my heart racing. "You both mentioned her like she matters, and if she does, I need to know why."

Brad exchanged a quick glance with Jonathan, a silent conversation passing between them that left me feeling more isolated than ever. The weight of their scrutiny made my skin prickle.

"Jessica," Brad said finally, his voice steady but cautious, "Mia's just someone from your past. Someone who cares about you." He hesitated, clearly measuring his words. "But right now, we need to focus on you."

I crossed my arms tightly over my chest, irritation bubbling within me. "What's happening? I don't want to be some pawn in this twisted game anymore." My voice shook slightly, revealing the fear lurking beneath my bravado.

"She was meant to be a surprise," Jonathan finally exclaimed. "It's your Mia, your friend. She's at the estate, waiting for you."

My heart raced at Brad's words, the realization crashing over me like a tidal wave. Mia was here? My friend, my ally, someone who knew the depths of my struggles? "She's at the estate?" I repeated, trying to process the shock. "Why didn't you tell me sooner?"

Brad opened his mouth but paused, searching for the right words. Jonathan stepped in. "We couldn't. But now we need to move quickly."

I felt a surge of urgency coursing through me. Without another thought, I darted into my room, scanning my closet frantically. My hands trembled as

I rifled through the hangers, pulling out a flowy blue dress that reminded me of summer skies and carefree days. It felt like a lifeline—something familiar amid the chaos.

I flung it onto my bed and snatched up a few necessities—a notebook and pen to capture the thoughts that spiraled ceaselessly in my head, something to anchor me. Each object carried significance, memories binding me to a feeling of stability.

"Jessica," Brad's voice broke through my concentration as he peeked into the room. "We really have to go."

"I'm almost done!" I snapped back, tossing the last of my items into a small bag and slinging it over my shoulder.

As I stepped back into the main area, Jonathan flanked one side while Brad took the other, both men urging me toward a narrow service stairwell that twisted down into darkness. My heart thudded in sync with our hurried footsteps, anxiety prickling at my skin.

They ushered me out a backdoor that creaked ominously on its hinges before leading us into the dimly lit alley behind the building. The air felt heavy with tension as we rounded corners cautiously until we reached Jonathan's car parked just beyond a flickering streetlight.

"Get in," Jonathan instructed as he opened the passenger door for me. I slid inside but barely had time to buckle up before there was an earth-shattering explosion. A deafening roar filled my ears as flames erupted just ten feet ahead of us, consuming a car in an inferno of fire and smoke.

Time slowed as I stared wide-eyed at the chaos unfolding before me, panic tightening around my throat like a vice grip while pieces of debris flew past us in wild arcs.

Chapter 23

Jessica

The explosion echoed in my ears, a thunderous roar that shook the ground beneath us. I barely registered Jonathan slamming the car door shut before he dove into the driver's seat, his face a mask of determination that spoke volumes about the urgency of our situation.

Brad slid into the backseat behind me, his eyes darting out the window, scanning every shadow as if it might harbor danger. I could see the tension radiating from him, the way his jaw clenched tightly and his breath quickened, mirroring the frantic rhythm of my heart. Each second felt like an eternity, the adrenaline coursing through my veins igniting a sense of both fear and resolve.

"Hang on!" Jonathan shouted, his voice cutting through the chaos that still reverberated in my ears. With that, he slammed the accelerator to the floor, and the car lurched forward with a violent jolt that sent me pressing back into my seat. The tires screeched against the asphalt, a desperate cry for escape, as we shot away from the devastation that lay behind us, the smoke swirling ominously in our rearview mirror.

"That explosion wasn't random," Brad screamed, his voice tight with urgency as he gripped the edge of his seat, knuckles white against the fabric. I could feel the panic rising within me, a knot forming in my stomach as I glanced back, half-expecting another blast to follow us, a haunting reminder of the danger we were in.

I nodded, still grappling with the sudden turn of events. Fear gnawed at my insides like a hungry animal, but I couldn't let it paralyze me now. I had to stay focused, to keep my wits about me in this overwhelming moment of crisis.

Jonathan swerved onto a side street, his grip white- knuckled on the wheel as he navigated through narrow alleys and deserted roads, each turn jolting my nerves further. The uncertainty of our path weighed heavily on me, yet I had no choice but to trust him. He knew what he was doing—he had to.

"Stay low," Jonathan instructed sharply as we ducked beneath an overhanging awning, the world outside a blur of shadows and flickering streetlights. My heart raced in time with our erratic path, each bump in the road sending a shiver of dread through me.

"What do you think they want?" I asked breathlessly, glancing back at Brad, whose face reflected my own anxiety, his eyes wide with fear and determination.

"They're after power," he responded sharply, the gravity of his words chilling me to the bone. "And you're in their sights. Mr. Kline isn't fond of being challenged, and he wants to show you your place after what you did at that center." The weight of his words settled heavily in my chest, an anchor of dread as we took another sharp turn. We were moving in circles now—looping through unfamiliar neighborhoods as Jonathan tried to shake any potential pursuers off our tail.

My mind whirred with possibilities, each one more terrifying than the last, spiraling into a vortex of fear and uncertainty. The shadows around us felt alive, swirling in the corners of my vision, and I couldn't shake the gnawing sensation that we were being hunted.

"Do you think they know where we are?" I asked quietly, my voice barely above a whisper, feeling vulnerability wash over me like cold water, chilling me to the bone. The weight of our situation pressed down on me, constricting my chest and making it hard to breathe, as if the very air was thick with impending doom.

"They're always watching," Brad muttered darkly from behind me, his tone laced with grim reality. I could hear the tension in his voice, a reflection of the fear we both felt, and it sent a shiver down my spine, heightening my awareness of our precarious predicament.

Jonathan cursed under his breath as he veered left onto another unlit road that seemed to stretch endlessly into darkness, the uncertainty of what lay ahead pressing in on us. "I'm not stopping until we're far enough away," he declared firmly, his tone brooked no argument. "The estate is safe. We are safe there." The promise hung in the air, a flicker of hope in a moment shrouded in chaos.

The car surged onto the highway, the asphalt stretching endlessly ahead like a dark ribbon of possibility. The roar of the engine filled the air, drowning out the chaos that had erupted moments ago, a cacophony of fear and desperation that felt like a lifetime ago. I settled into my seat, my body still trembling from adrenaline and fear, yet a strange calm washed over me as we sped away from danger, the landscape blurring past us in a rush of shadows and muted colors.

"Jonathan," I began, my voice barely audible above the hum of the tires on pavement, "what now?" The uncertainty gnawed at me, a persistent ache deep in my stomach. Every turn had felt desperate, each second stretching longer than the last, and I couldn't help but feel like we were racing against time itself.

"We get to safety first," he replied with a reassuring nod, his eyes fixed on the road ahead, unwavering and determined. "Then we get you married." His words hung in the air, both a promise and a plan, and I couldn't help but feel a flicker of warmth at the thought, even amid the chaos.

Jonathan shifted in his seat beside me, glancing at Brad, who sat in the back, his face a mask of concentration. "How's everyone else holding up?" he asked, his tone holding a mix of concern and curiosity that pulled me back into the present, grounding me in the reality of our situation.

Brad took a moment to gather his thoughts before answering, his brow furrowing as he chose his words carefully. "I didn't get to meet any of them when I dropped off Mia," he said slowly, his voice steady but tinged with worry. "I was just focused on her. It was clear she couldn't stay at that holding facility after twenty-four hours." His gaze flicked briefly to mine before returning to the road, as if he could see the weight of my anxiety reflected in my eyes. "So, I contacted Mr. Dandin about bringing her home."

A wave of relief washed over me at the mention of Mia's name, my heart swelling with gratitude. "You brought her to the estate? That's great!" I exclaimed, my voice stronger now, grateful for any shred of good news in this storm of chaos. The thought of Mia safe with us filled me with a sense of hope I desperately needed.

"Yeah," Jonathan chimed in with a hint of pride, his smile a beacon of reassurance. "He did what had to be done. He will be a great addition to your staff."

"Just doing what I could," Brad replied modestly, though I could see how pleased he was by Jonathan's acknowledgment, a small spark of joy in the midst of our turbulent journey. He shifted in the backseat, and as we cruised down the highway, I leaned back against the seat, letting the vibration of the car soothe my frayed nerves while my thoughts drifted.

"What about the rest of them?" I asked cautiously, anxiety creeping back in as images of my friends flashed through my mind—Mia's laughter, Grace's reassuring smile, and the vibrant energy we shared felt like distant memories now, fading under the weight of uncertainty. "Will they be accepting of me coming into the house?"

"I cannot comment on that," Jonathan admitted with a sigh, his expression turning serious. "I made a promise." The gravity of his words settled heavily in the air, and I swallowed hard, feeling a wave of helplessness wash over me again. The thought of them facing whatever dangers awaited us while I sat here in relative safety twisted something deep inside me, a knot of guilt that I couldn't untie.

Brad turned slightly toward me, his expression earnest, a warmth radiating from him that was almost palpable. "They'll be okay, Jess," he assured me softly, as if sensing my unease, his voice a soothing balm against my rising panic.

I nodded slowly, but I couldn't shake off the worry gnawing at my insides as we sped into an uncertain future together on that highway, the world outside cloaked in darkness, yet filled with the flickering lights of hope.

I jolted awake as the car turned onto a long gravel driveway, the crunch of stones beneath the tires pulling me from the depths of my restless sleep. My heart raced, pounding against my ribcage as I blinked against the darkness, struggling to orient myself in the unfamiliar surroundings. The faint glow from the dashboard cast eerie shadows across the interior, heightening my sense of disorientation. I could hear Jonathan's voice, low and steady, discussing something with Brad, but their words faded into the background. All I could focus on was the urgency in my chest, an anxious flutter that urged me to piece together what was happening. The lingering remnants of my dreams clung to me like cobwebs, and I fought to shake them off as I tried to make sense of my reality.

The headlights illuminated a towering gate as Jonathan slowed to a stop, the sound of gravel crunching beneath the tires punctuating the stillness. He punched a code into the keypad, and I held my breath in anticipation, watching with wide eyes as the heavy gate swung open with a creak that echoed in the quiet of the night. It felt like a portal to another world—one where I could finally breathe freely, away from the weight of expectations and fears that had been pressing down on me.

We drove for what felt like ages, the landscape shifting with every turn, my heart racing and anticipation building with each passing moment. Finally, a large white mansion emerged from the darkness, its elegant structure illuminated by the moonlight. It loomed ahead, majestic and serene, standing proud against the backdrop of an ink-black sky. I couldn't help but marvel at its grandeur; it looked almost ethereal under the full moon's glow, like something out of a dream I had long since forgotten.

As we pulled closer, my pulse quickened when two figures emerged from the shadows at the front door. My heart leaped when I recognized Mia first—her familiar silhouette framed by the soft light spilling from inside the mansion, exuding an energy that was impossible to ignore. Beside her stood a n ally I never thought I'd see again, Carolynn, her vibrant presence equally striking against the night, with her soft blue eyes sparkling with excitement.

Before Jonathan even fully stopped the car, I flung open my door and leapt out into the cool night air, the rush of freedom washing over me like a tide.

"Mia!" I cried out, tears spilling down my cheeks as I rushed into her arms. The warmth enveloped me like a safety blanket, her presence washing away some of my fears and uncertainties.

"Jessica!" she exclaimed, holding me tightly as if she were afraid I'd vanish again. "I was so worried about you!"

As I looked up to greet Carolynn next, ready to share this moment of reunion with her too, my eyes widened at an unexpected sight: Jonathan leaning down to kiss her passionately right there on the front steps of Dandin Estate.

The joy of seeing Mia mingled with surprise at their display of affection—a mixture that left me momentarily speechless as reality settled around us like fog creeping in from nowhere.

Mia tugged at my hand, gently guiding me toward the front door as if to pull me away from the unexpected scene unfolding before us. "Let them be," she said with a playful smile, "they're just young and in love."

"But won't Mr. Dandin be upset if he finds them?" I asked, my curiosity piquing as I wondered where my future husband might be hiding amidst all this. The thought of this mystery man filled me with a mix of fear and anxious anticipation.

Mia chuckled softly, her laughter a comforting sound that eased my worries. "You'll meet him at your breakfast wedding ceremony tomorrow," she reassured me, her eyes sparkling with mischief and joy. "Now, let's get you some rest so you can look absolutely stunning." I couldn't help but feel a flutter of hope at the prospect of what was to come, even as I glanced back at Carolynn and Jonathan, their moment of sweet intimacy lingering in my mind.

Chapter 24

Jessica

I awoke to soft sunlight streaming through the sheer curtains, casting a warm glow across the room. My surroundings were grand yet strangely basic—white walls adorned with simple, unadorned frames and a large, polished wooden bed that felt both inviting and foreign. I lay there for a moment, trying to shake off the remnants of sleep while my heart raced with memories of the night before. A knock on the door startled me from my thoughts, jolting me back to reality.

"Jess? It's time to get up!" Mia's cheerful voice filtered through the wood, a welcome sound that sliced through the morning fog and pulled me from the cocoon of my blankets. I could practically feel her infectious energy radiating through the door.

I swung my legs over the side of the bed, feeling the coolness of the polished floor beneath my feet, a stark contrast to the warmth of my bed. Taking a deep breath to shake off the remnants of sleep, I opened the door and was immediately met by Mia's bright smile and Carolynn's encouraging nod, both of which felt like a burst of sunshine.

"You look like you've seen a ghost!" Mia teased, her laughter echoing in the hallway as she pushed her way into the room, her enthusiasm spilling over. "Let's get you ready! Big day ahead!" Her words hung in the air, heavy with promise and possibility.

Carolynn followed behind her, an armful of clothes and accessories that made my head spin with their vibrant colors and textures. "We don't have much time," she said, her tone laced with an air of urgency as she began rifling through the garments, already assessing what might work best for me. I could see the determination in her soft blue eyes, as if she knew today was not just any day.

Mia grabbed my hand, her grip reassuring, and led me toward a large mirror that reflected not just our images but also the shared excitement—and maybe some nerves—bubbling beneath the surface about what was coming. I took a moment to glance at our reflections, a trio of hopeful faces ready to face whatever the day had in store.

As they rifled through options, I caught a glimpse of myself in the mirror: a blend of uncertainty and determination swirling within me, ready to confront whatever awaited.

"First things first," Carolynn said, her fingers brushing back my hair with a deftness that surprised me. She wove it into an elegant style, one that made me feel somewhat regal, as if I were stepping into a grand tale. "You need to look perfect for your husband-to- be."

"Right," I murmured, my mind drifting into a fog of thoughts about who this man might be. I pondered how he would fit into the tapestry of my life—or perhaps more pressing, how I would fit into his. The weight of the unknown sat heavy on my shoulders, but there was a flicker of hope igniting within me, urging me to embrace this new chapter.

Mia selected a flowing white dress from the pile—a gown that seemed almost ethereal in its simplicity yet striking enough to evoke an air of importance. "This one! It's gorgeous." She held it up against me, her eyes sparkling with enthusiasm.

As they helped me slip into the dress, I felt an odd mix of emotions swirling within me: apprehension about what was to come mingled with excitement at being surrounded by friends who genuinely cared about me.

"You'll be stunning," Carolynn assured as she adjusted the neckline carefully. "Just remember to breathe."

With each passing moment, I could feel their energy lifting mine; their camaraderie wrapped around me like a warm blanket as they prepped me for this new chapter of my life.

Connor

The garden unfolded before me, a vibrant tapestry of colors and scents that I had rushed to cultivate for today. Each flower, carefully chosen, reflected the hopes I harbored for Jessica, the girl who consumed my thoughts. The bright yellows danced in the sunlight, while deep blues swayed gently in the breeze, creating a symphony of hues that filled my heart with anticipation. I inhaled deeply, letting the fresh fragrance anchor me in this precious moment.

Here, amidst the blooming petals, this place had become our sanctuary—a refuge from the chaos that seemed to surround us at every turn, a space where dreams felt just a little closer to reality.

Brad appeared first, his usual easy smile replaced with a seriousness that suited the occasion, as if the weight of the moment pressed down upon him. He stepped beside me, hands clasped together in front of him, a gesture that signified he was preparing for something monumental—something that would change everything.

"Connor, she's ready," he announced, his voice steady but low, almost reverent. "Mia and Carolynn are with her."

I nodded, my heart racing at the thought of Jessica walking toward me in that stunning dress, the anticipation mingling with a mix of excitement and nerves. Images of her laughter and the way her blue eyes sparkled filled my mind, heightening the intensity of the moment. I could almost see her now, radiant and full of life, stepping into the light where I stood waiting, ready to embrace whatever fate had in store for us.

Jonathan and Shane joined us moments later, their expressions mirroring my own blend of excitement and anxiety. I could see the eagerness in their eyes, a reflection of the weight of the moment that loomed ahead.

"Everything's set," Jonathan confirmed, adjusting his tie with a touch of nervous precision. "Just need to get into position." His voice held a steady confidence, but I knew he felt the stakes as acutely as I did.

Shane chuckled softly, his laughter slicing through the tension that had settled over us like a heavy fog. "You look like you're about to face down a battalion instead of marrying the woman you've moved heavens and earth for." His light-hearted jab, delivered with that familiar grin, brought a flicker of relief to my chest, even as my heart raced at the thought of what lay ahead. I could hardly wrap my mind around the magnitude of this moment, the weight of what I was about to commit to. But Shane's humor reminded me that amidst the chaos, there was still joy to be found.

"Funny," I shot him a grin, but the twist in my stomach reminded me of the gravity of the situation. "You forget, she's never met me." The weight of that reality settled around us, a reminder that this moment was not just about love; it was about courage, hope, and the leap into the unknown that awaited us both.

Brad stepped forward, taking charge as the officiant. "Let's get this started then." His presence steadied me; I needed someone who understood the weight of this moment.

As we lined up, I caught sight of Mia and Carolynn guiding Jessica through the entrance, which was adorned with blossoms and ribbons that danced gently in the soft breeze. My breath caught in my throat as she appeared—radiant, filled with an ethereal grace that seemed almost otherworldly.

Her wedding dress was a masterpiece, cascading down her petite frame in delicate layers of silk that caught the light, shimmering as she moved. Her long brown hair was styled elegantly, cascading in soft waves that framed her face and spilled over her shoulders, while a delicate veil adorned with lace edged her hair, adding just the right touch of elegance. The makeup was subtle yet enhancing, highlighting her striking blue eyes that sparkled with a mix of excitement and trepidation. A hint of blush warmed her cheeks, making her look even more beautiful, as if she were radiating from within. In that moment, she was not just my Jessica; she was a vision of hope and love, stepping into a future that, despite the uncertainty, felt filled with promise.

"Remember Roger and Clara?" I murmured to myself as Brad began his opening words. Their story resonated within me like a gentle echo of my own feelings for Jessica—love born from resilience amidst oppression.

I watched Jessica step closer, her eyes wide yet full of determination.

"When they faced their battles," I continued in my mind while Brad spoke of love's promise, "they knew they had to fight not just for themselves but for those they loved."

And here I was, ready to make my vow—to love and care for Jessica fiercely while promising to change this world that sought to tear us apart.

"Today is about you two," Brad said now, looking between us as he gestured toward Jessica and me. The garden held its breath in anticipation as we prepared to step into our shared future together.

As Jessica stepped closer, her eyes shimmering with a mix of hope and uncertainty, I felt an urge to ground her in something solid, something we both understood. "You know," I began, my voice low enough for only her to hear, "Roger and Clara's story has always inspired me."

She tilted her head slightly, a spark of curiosity igniting in those brilliant blue eyes.

"My Uncle Roger was always this force," I continued, my thoughts drifting back to the stories I cherished about my uncle and his first wife. "He was determined to change the world. He fought against the centers long before most of us even realized how important it was to resist." I could see the interest deepen in Jessica's expression; she leaned in a little closer, hanging on my words as if they were lifelines.

"And your Aunt Clara? She was his inspiration," I added. "She believed in hope when everyone else seemed ready to give up. They met under the worst circumstances—two souls navigating a system designed to crush dreams. But instead of falling apart, they became stronger together."

Jessica's gaze softened as she listened intently.

"She wanted to change the world for someone who mattered more to her than the world itself," A knot formed in my throat; their story wasn't just history; it felt like a warning.

"You" I said firmly, meeting Jessica's gaze with determination. "She wanted to change the world for you."

"You knew my Aunt Clara?" she asked quietly, her voice barely above a whisper.

I hesitated for a moment, gathering my thoughts. "I never met her, but my Uncle told me stories. They had plans to change the world, to fight back and stop the horrible things going on" The pride I felt for them swelled within me like an unquenchable flame.

"They showed that love could thrive even in the darkest times," I said, leaning closer so only she could hear. "Their love wasn't just about them; it was about everyone they could save."

As those words hung between us, I could feel the weight of our situation settling in once more—the stakes were higher than ever before—but sharing their story felt like breathing life into our own struggle against the chaos surrounding us.

The garden shimmered with the soft light of the late morning sun, and as I looked into Jessica's eyes, I felt an overwhelming surge of commitment. This was our moment—a promise sealed in the beauty of nature and the weight of our shared experiences.

"Jessica," I began, my voice steady but full of emotion. "From this day forward, I devote myself to loving you for the rest of my life." The words felt monumental as they left my lips, a vow that wrapped around us like a protective cloak.

She searched my eyes, her expression a mixture of hope and disbelief. "You mean that?" she asked softly, almost as if she needed reassurance that such devotion could exist amidst the chaos surrounding us.

"I do," I affirmed, feeling every syllable resonate within me. "I will fight for you. Not just to protect you but to change everything that's wrong in this world. No one else should ever have to endure what you've gone through." The conviction surged through me like wildfire. Each word ignited a spark within me—an unwavering determination that settled into my bones.

Her gaze held mine, and I could see her processing my promise. There was something profound about sharing this commitment with her here in this garden, where love bloomed amidst despair.

"I don't want you to fight alone," she said quietly, her voice thick with emotion. "It's not just about me."

"I know," I replied firmly. "It's about all of you—about everyone suffering under this oppressive system. Together, we'll find a way to break the system" The weight of responsibility hung heavy on my shoulders, but it felt right; it felt like destiny calling me to action.

As I spoke, memories flooded back—the countless conversations with my uncle Roger about his dreams for a better world. Those discussions fueled the fire within me now; they inspired me to make our struggles matter beyond ourselves.

"Together," I continued, holding her gaze with intensity. "We can be more than just hopeful—we can become warriors for change."

I reached out and gently took her hands in mine, feeling the warmth radiate between us as if our hearts beat in unison. "I promise to stand by your side through every challenge we face," I declared, squeezing her hands slightly as if sealing our pact with an unbreakable bond.

As I held Jessica's hands, the weight of the moment pressed against my chest. Her blue eyes shimmered with something profound, a mix of hope and vulnerability that pulled me deeper into this shared connection. I could see her mind racing, processing everything—the chaos we had endured and the path that lay ahead.

"I know we just met," she began, her voice steady yet soft, almost hesitant as if she was still searching for the right words. "I know our circumstances are... complicated." She paused, taking a breath that seemed to gather all the courage she had. "But your promise means more to me than you can imagine."

My heart raced as she continued, the anticipation hanging thick in the air between us.

"I've spent so long feeling powerless—like I'm just another pawn in a game played by those who don't care about us," she confessed, her voice wavering slightly. "But you… You make me feel like there's a chance—like I could be more than what they want me to be."

I squeezed her hands tighter, feeling a rush of determination surge through me. This was it—the spark that could ignite a fire against everything that sought to bind us.

"I want to fight alongside you," she declared, her gaze unwavering now. "Not just for myself but for everyone trapped in this cruel system. For Mia, for Grace… for everyone who's ever felt hopeless."

Her passion lit something inside me, an unyielding fire that resonated with my own desire to protect not just her but every soul affected by this oppressive regime.

"I vow," she stated, her tone shifting to something softer but resolute. "to stand with you—through every challenge we face together."

The sincerity in her voice wrapped around my heart like an embrace. I felt an overwhelming rush of emotions—a cocktail of hope and defiance flooding my veins.

"I vow to fight back against this system with everything I have," she continued. "To refuse to let them dictate our worth or our futures."

As those words poured from her lips, I couldn't help but feel a swell of pride swell within me; here was this incredible woman promising strength and resilience when all odds seemed stacked against us.

In that moment, standing in the garden filled with blooms and dreams intertwined with reality, we became something more than ourselves—we became partners in this fight against injustice.

Brad stood before us, his expression a blend of reverence and excitement. The garden buzzed with an air of anticipation, the vibrant colors around us seeming to echo the moment's significance.

"Today," he began, his voice steady and warm, "we gather to witness not just a union but a powerful testament to resilience." He gestured between Jessica and me, and I could feel the warmth of her hand in mine as she squeezed gently, grounding me in this whirlwind of emotions. "Connor and Jessica have chosen to forge their own path in a world that seeks to divide them."

I glanced at Jessica, her eyes shimmering with determination. I wanted nothing more than to protect that fire within her.

Brad continued, his words flowing like a gentle river, "In their commitment to one another lies hope for all of us. Together, they embody strength and courage—a beacon in these dark times." He paused for a moment, letting his gaze sweep over our small gathering. I could see nods of agreement from those present—Mia standing nearby with an encouraging smile,

Carolynn beaming with pride.

"They remind us that love can thrive even in adversity," Brad said softly. "As we witness this union today, we are reminded how blessed we all are to share this journey with them."

His voice rose slightly as he reached the ceremony's climax. "And so, by the power vested in me," he declared with an air of authority, "I now pronounce you husband and wife."

The words hung in the air like a spell cast upon us.

"Connor," Brad turned toward me with an inviting smile. "You may kiss your bride."

A rush of exhilaration surged through me at that moment—the culmination of everything we had fought for distilled into this singular act. I leaned closer to Jessica, who looked up at me with wide eyes filled with joy and something deeper—an understanding that transcended words.

With a gentle touch on her cheek, I leaned in and pressed my lips against hers. Time slowed as our surroundings faded into oblivion; it was just us—a promise sealed by our kiss amidst blooming flowers and whispered vows of defiance against the world outside.

As we broke apart, laughter erupted from our friends around us—a chorus of joy that rang out like music in the air—and my heart swelled at what lay ahead.

Chapter 25

Jessica

A month had passed since the whirlwind of our wedding, and here I stood in the kitchen, surveying the vibrant chaos that was now our home. The walls echoed with laughter, a symphony of joy that wrapped around me like a warm embrace, while the mouth-watering scent of barbecue wafted in from the backyard, teasing my senses with its savory allure. I felt a swell of pride as I admired my handiwork—each room infused with color and warmth, a stark contrast to the sterile environments we had endured for so long. The soft hues and eclectic decorations reflected not only my personality but also the love that filled this space. It was a sanctuary, a place where memories were being forged, free from the constraints of the past that had haunted us for so long.

Connor strolled in, his eyes bright and full of life, and I couldn't help but marvel at how surreal it felt that I had only met him a month ago. It was hard to believe that just a few short weeks had transformed my world so completely, bringing someone so vibrant and passionate into my life. The memory of our first encounter lingered in my mind, a whirlwind of emotions that had sparked something within me that I never knew existed. Here he was now, effortlessly filling the room with his energy, and I found myself captivated all over again, wondering how fate could weave such a beautiful tapestry in such a brief span of time.

"Looks amazing, Jess," he said, leaning against the doorframe with that familiar grin that always sent butterflies dancing in my stomach, a reminder of the excitement he brought into my life.

I turned to him, my heart fluttering at his praise, feeling a warmth spread through me, igniting a sense of belonging deep within. "You really think so? I wanted it to feel… like home." My voice was tinged with a hint of vulnerability, reflecting the effort I'd put into making this space a true reflection of myself, a testament to the journey we had undertaken together.

"It does," he replied softly, his eyes sparkling with sincerity as he stepped closer, closing the distance between us. He wrapped an arm around my shoulders, pulling me gently against him, grounding me in the moment. "It feels like you." His words wrapped around me like a comforting blanket, and in that moment, I couldn't help but feel that maybe, just maybe, I was exactly where I was meant to be.

The sound of sizzling meat pulled me back into the moment, wrapping around me like a warm embrace. Outside, the air was filled with laughter, mingling effortlessly with the clinking of utensils as our friends gathered for a summer barbecue. Meg and Jake had seamlessly joined our staff, their vibrant chemistry lighting up even the most mundane tasks. Their playful banter infused the atmosphere with a sense of ease that made everything feel lighter, more joyful.

We had fought hard to bring them into our circle after their own struggles, and it felt like a small victory worth celebrating. Yet, amid the laughter and camaraderie, Annie and Aaron lingered in my thoughts like ghosts—elusive figures lost to the shadows of the past, their absence a stark reminder of the battles we couldn't win. Connor and I had spent many long nights trying to hunt down where they were taken, but whatever their father had lined up for them was outside of even Connor's reach.

"Have you seen Shane?" I asked Connor as we made our way toward the patio, the anticipation of the gathering buzzing in the air, electrifying my senses.

"He's probably watching those feeds again," he chuckled, the sound warm and familiar, a melody that filled me with comfort. "I swear he thinks he's some sort of secret agent now, searching for hidden treasures among the chaos."

I smiled at that image; it perfectly captured Shane's relentless spirit. He was always on the lookout, determined to find potential staff members among those still in need, convinced that every glimmer of hope could be transformed into something meaningful. He'd become a beacon of determination for so many of us.

The sun hung high in the sky, casting a golden hue over everything as we stepped outside. The yard buzzed with excitement—Carolynn expertly flipped burgers on the grill, the mouthwatering aroma wafting through the air, while Jonathan prepared drinks at a nearby table, his laughter mingling with the sounds of joy around us. My heart swelled at the sight of them together; they looked so happy, a testament to the camaraderie we had built through our trials. Then, as if sensing my gaze, Carolynn turned and caught my eye, her smile radiant and infectious, lifting my spirits even higher.

"Hey! Everyone!" she shouted over the chatter, her voice bursting with energy, cutting through the joyful noise that surrounded us like a beacon, drawing attention and excitement toward her.

"What's up?" I asked, moving closer, my curiosity piqued as I sensed something big was coming. The air crackled with anticipation, and I could feel the excitement building among our friends, each heartbeat matching the pulse of the moment.

Jonathan stepped forward beside her, grinning ear to ear, his joy infectious, and I couldn't help but mirror his smile, feeling the thrill of shared secrets. "We have an announcement!" His enthusiasm was palpable, and I could feel the tension of anticipation rising, tightening my chest with excitement.

A hush fell over our friends as they leaned in expectantly, their faces a mix of intrigue and excitement. I could see the glimmer of hope in their eyes, each of us drawn in by the promise of something wonderful, ready to celebrate whatever news was about to unfold.

Carolynn placed a hand on her stomach, her smile radiant and full of warmth, illuminating the space around her. "We're expecting a baby!" The words hung in the air, and for a moment, time seemed to stand still as the reality of her announcement settled over us, sparking a wave of cheers and congratulations that erupted like fireworks.

Cheers erupted around us, followed by applause and warm embraces all around. My heart raced—my friends were starting families; life was shifting into something new yet hopeful, a beautiful evolution of our shared experiences.

Amidst all this joy, I glanced toward Brad and Mia across the yard, their laughter carrying on the breeze like music, a harmonious blend of happiness. Something blossomed there too—an unexpected connection that filled me with warmth, a reminder that even in the midst of our struggles, love had the power to thrive.

I stood at the edge of the patio, my heart still racing from Carolynn's announcement, when I felt a familiar presence behind me. Connor's warmth enveloped me as he slipped his arms around my waist, resting his chin on my shoulder, grounding me amidst the whirlwind of emotions swirling around us.

"Did you hear the news?" he asked, his voice laced with playful excitement that instantly lifted my spirits like a balloon rising into the sky.

I turned slightly to look into his eyes, which sparkled with mischief, a twinkle that always made my heart skip a beat in a way I had never experienced

before. "Of course! It's incredible. They're going to be amazing parents," I replied, feeling a swell of joy for my friends as I imagined the beautiful life they would create together, filled with laughter, love, and endless possibilities.

Connor chuckled softly, a warm sound that wrapped around me like a comforting blanket, then leaned closer, whispering conspiratorially as if sharing a delicious secret meant only for my ears. "Now that all our staff have moved out of the house and into the staff houses... maybe it'll be our turn next."

I laughed, shaking my head at the audacious thought, a mixture of amusement and disbelief dancing through me. "First, we need to fix this world before we even think about babies," I replied, my tone growing serious as I considered the weighty implications of bringing new life into such a turbulent environment, a world still grappling with its many injustices, where hope often felt like a flickering candle in the wind.

"Who says we can't have both?" he challenged lightly, though I sensed the deeper question lurking beneath his words, a question that hung in the air between us like a promise unspoken.

I paused for a moment, absorbing what he had said. "We need to make it safe for them first." My heart felt heavy at the thought of innocent children navigating this broken world filled with uncertainty and danger, a world I desperately wished to change.

"Safe?" Connor mused thoughtfully, his brows furrowing as he pondered my words. "And how do you propose we do that?"

I turned fully to face him now, letting go of my earlier thoughts for just a moment, allowing his presence to steady me. "Well," I started slowly, looking deep into his eyes, searching for understanding. "It starts with people like us taking a stand."

He raised an eyebrow, clearly intrigued by my conviction. "People like us?"

"Yeah," I replied confidently, feeling a surge of determination. "You're my knight in shining armor— leading the charge against all this injustice." It felt good to say it aloud, to frame our shared mission in such a bold and hopeful way.

A smile crept across Connor's face as he processed my words, amusement dancing in his eyes. "Knight in shining armor? That's a bit dramatic, don't you think?"

"Not at all!" I insisted, my voice rising with conviction, fueled by the passion that burned within me. "You've fought for me—fought for all of us—and that makes you exactly that."

His expression softened as he regarded me seriously, a warmth radiating from him that made me feel like we could take on the world together. "Then together, we'll create a future where those babies can thrive without fear," he said, and in that moment, I felt a glimmer of hope for what lay ahead.

ABOUT THE AUTHOR

Tara Howard is a devoted wife and proud mother of two who finds joy in both the everyday chaos of family life and the quiet moments of creative escape. A true lover of stories, she can often be found curled up with a book, especially when the sound of ocean waves provides the perfect backdrop. Reading by the beach is one of her greatest pleasures, as is writing while on vacation, where the change of scenery fuels her imagination and transports her into new worlds.

Tara has always been drawn to the magic of storytelling, particularly in the realm of fantasy, where anything is possible and adventure awaits around every corner. She believes in the power of books to transport, inspire, and heal, and she strives to create stories that offer readers the same kind of escape she cherishes.

When she's not writing or reading, Tara enjoys spending time with her family, making cherished memories with her husband and children as well as her parents and extended family including her many nieces and nephews. She also adores her two dogs, who bring constant love and companionship to her home.

Whether she's at home with her loved ones, exploring a new destination, or dreaming up her next novel, Tara remains a firm believer in the beauty of true love and the happily-ever-afters that make life—and fiction—so enchanting.